Henry Esmond

A Life's Hazard or the Outlaw of Wentworth Waste

Vol. III

Henry Esmond

A Life's Hazard or the Outlaw of Wentworth Waste
Vol. III

ISBN/EAN: 9783744666855

Printed in Europe, USA, Canada, Australia, Japan

Cover: Foto ©Andreas Hilbeck / pixelio.de

More available books at **www.hansebooks.com**

A LIFE'S HAZARD;

OR,

THE OUTLAW OF WENTWORTH WASTE.

By HENRY ESMOND.

IN THREE VOLUMES.

VOL. III.

London :

SAMPSON LOW, MARSTON, SEARLE, & RIVINGTON,

CROWN BUILDINGS, 188, FLEET STREET.

1878.

A LIFE'S HAZARD;

OR,

THE OUTLAW OF WENTWORTH WASTE.

CHAPTER I.

" I can't fathom it," said the captain of
the good ship the " Amber Wave," bound
from Liverpool to New York; " these Irish
baffle me. First we are told to look out
for suspicious craft, and especially two
men who have escaped from prison; these
we fail to fall in with, but instead we
tackle a pair of somebodies, taking them on
board, when they immediately run foul of
all our reckonings, one dying, the other
offering any money to get away and leave
us to bury the dead."

The foregoing remarks were addressed to the first officer, who, with the captain, was doing a regulation stroll along the poop before turning in for the night.

"They are evidently of the well-to-do class, and must have suffered terribly before we took them in tow," suggested the subordinate to his superior.

"Yes, I pity her; but why does he drag astern, while although unable to run many more knots this side of the channel, she keeps every sail set to get spliced before slipping her cable?"

"You think she won't live, sir?"

"Not much longer," was decisively answered.

"It is strange to hail a pilot when running into the last port," musingly observed the younger man.

"Yes," replied the captain, "but she seems to be a fair sailer after all, and, as she says, they were to be mainbraced at once; why does he turn away now, leaving her to lurch out of her scupper alone? Upon my word," he vehemently added, "in the morning I will jam him close in the wind until I know more of the land-shark," whereupon both sought the repose of their respective cabins.

The "Amber Wave" was a full-rigged ship, having a large cargo of merchandise, and very few passengers. She was now several days out, but with head winds, shortened sails, and battened holds, made little way, rolling about amid the giddy waves like a massive, huge tub.

All the outward vessels of the day were charged to watch the seashore of Ireland for suspicious craft, which signified treason or smuggling, and to permit of no passengers being taken on board who could not satisfactorily account for themselves, it often happening that these slow sailing-ships were accosted by a small boat, and a stranger sent on deck, who, on payment of the passage-money, was gladly welcomed, although the person might have been a fugitive from justice.

While off the dangerous Carnsore Point at Wexford, the "Amber Wave" being hove to in a raging tempest, the three masts and gaff topsail of a water-logged barque came in sight, hoisting signals of distress, which were immediately responded to by Captain Nicholson, a fearless old salt.

" Man the boat," he ordered resolutely, " and pull away my lads."

" Ay, ay, sir," rose up cheerily from the willing Jack-tar, and already the pinnace went ploughing through the ruthless waves on the dangerous enterprise.

The sea was dashing tumultuously

around the derelict, driving lifelessly through the watery element.

That brave crew, however, would not forsake her, but pointed out to their intended rescuers the forms of a young man and a woman, who, in hopeless wretchedness and despondency, looked on at what was passing, powerless to interfere.

"Heigho! bad cargo," muttered the boatswain, adding aloud, "where do they hail from?"

"Don't know, mate, some days ago saved them from drowning. She can't live, take them on board, pay you well," answered from stentorian lungs.

"Make fast the hawser and move forward if you can," was replied, the pinnace being impelled alongside the floating wreck. The process of getting the castaways into the boat was long and dangerous, one of them having to be slung almost roughly from the davits in cocoa matting. However, this was safely accomplished, and they reached the "Amber Wave" after a heavy pull of the eight steady united oars.

The kindly nature of Captain Nicholson at once revealed itself, providing the strangers with every item of comfort that his vessel could possibly yield, while postponing the usual questions, waiting for a favourable opportunity to receive an account of their misadventure.

Despite the adverse weather, baffling every calculation, the two wanderers grew better, he of the sterner sex especially, but the captain was rudely shocked on the day when we first read of him to be summoned to the bedside of the recovering lady, who suddenly announced her conviction that she was dying, and that she wanted him to perform the ceremony of marriage between herself and her rescued companion, even while yet she lived, as they themselves had resolved, having been long betrothed. To the officer's reply that it was only in very rare instances he exercised such unusual functions, and that he hoped she would be better when the "roughish weather settled a bit," she answered pathetically,—

"What more extreme case have you ever found than mine? I cannot possibly survive many hours."

And when the bluff old sailor closely regarded her, the unusual deathlike expression of that face which he had not observed previously seemed to justify the estimate she had formed as to her duration of life.

"It is the love of years, do not refuse a dying girl," was so piteously urged that Captain Nicholson left the darkened cabin, resolved on complying with her hallowed request, and sought out the object of her affections, to arrange for the nuptial proceeding; but the answer of this gentleman proved the reverse of satisfactory.

"Yes, they were engaged, although not for years, and he remembered a conditional marriage project, but he could not see the wisdom of being wed to a dying woman; better to postpone it, she might live after all," formed the gist of his observations to the master of the "Amber Wave," whose opinion thereupon we have just recorded, while walking the poop with the chief mate preparatory to seeking the oblivion of his pillow.

That night wore on tranquilly, the good ship making amends for past delay, although in so doing she veered slightly out of her reckoning, drifting westward; but the subsidence of the long prevailing storm was the theme for mutual congratu-

lations which extended even to the exhausted lady in her cosey berth. At breakfast it was noticed that the strange gentleman spoke less than ever, and seemed
more reserved, although at all times his
manner to the crew had been taciturn and
repelling.

The foot of the subordinate became
impinged upon that of his superior under
the table, who, looking up to ascertain its
cause, understood the wink, mutely direct-
ing him to watch the passenger playing
with his unused knife, while eagerly looking upon the well-supplied, untasted plate.

The captain answered meaningly with
knowing expressive eyes, saying aloud,—

" We are in for a spell of fine weather."

" Yes," observed his chief, " the wind
has hauled round, and stands to force
some quick sailing."

" Where are we now ? "

This was the first time the stranger had spoken during the repast.

"On board ship," quickly replied the captain, laughing.

The questioner smiled also, resuming,—

"That I know, but I meant to ask what part of the coast are we near?"

"Galway, sir."

"I will give you five hundred guineas to place me on land," the previous speaker exclaimed with an energy of passion and hopefulness unexpected and unlooked for.

The son of Neptune was very composed as he answered,—

"There is one condition alone on which I will put you ashore for a fifth of the sum offered."

"Name it!"

"With your wife, only."

"But she cannot survive," was observed in a tone of half-triumph.

"She will die easier there than on board ship," curtly retorted the aged officer.

"A dead woman is not much of an acquisition anywhere," the unknown uttered sententiously.

"And a false living husband is but too often a shameless, undying scar on the memory of a good, honest wife."

The captain now warmly disliked the calculating, silent young man before him, and heatedly following up his last words added,—

"I will keep at sea three months before we make New York, if it will prevent your leaving that girl to die among strangers."

"Place me on land, I will take her with me, and still give you five hundred guineas."

"The offer sounds fair, and this moment we will ask her to accept it, provided she is able to be sent on shore," though the honest sailor inwardly thought, " I would not trust the lubber while he could put his hand into his pocket and withdraw it again."

The ship held on at a rattling speed, cutting through the low swells which slunk away at her approach, while the bright rays of the brighter sun were reflected from the manifold ruddy objects on the receding shore.

They now entered the invalid's apartment, the bluff salt taking the patient's hand, who seemed wan and ghastly, saying,—

" You will be better, my dear, and I shall put you ashore in less than two hours."

" Then," she sadly sighed, "you will not marry us," casting a look of pleading force towards her *fiancé*, who stood hat in hand calmly watching her.

" I would," embarrassingly observed the captain, "but—"

" It will be better to wait until we land," interposed the young man.

" Oh! take me to sea, sir, and hide me in the deep wave," exclaimed the failing lady.

An almost preternatural silence followed the unwonted appeal, during which the bronzed sailor deeply pitied the suffering girl for thinking of one so unwilling to become her husband, while the latter was cautiously communing within himself.

" Better to undergo the farce, and leave her to die, than imperil heaven knows what tossing about at the mercy of this confounded fellow and his ship."

" Fanny, are you content to remain on board trying to recover while continuing the voyage, sooner than risk being moved now, provided this gentleman unites us ?"

"Make me the happy wife you promised, and resign me to my destiny," was responded in very weak tones.

"You will proceed to America, and permit of my going on shore to arrange urgent affairs; I shall follow you by the very next vessel."

"I will go to my grave content when we are married; it is all I ask."

"Captain," the stranger demanded in a a decided tone, "perform the service."

"It is an unnatural contract," thought the honest mariner, "but she will soon be at rest, apart from the scoundrel."

"Ship ahoy!" was now heard from the side of the vessel.

"What is the matter?" shouted the mate, jumping on to the taffrail, as a small boat came rowing in their wake.

"Where are ye bound for?" rose up from the oarsmen.

" New York."

" That'll do—there's two gintlemin
wants to thravel be ye, hould an till they
git up."

" I can't admit any one without the
captain's permission."

" Shure thin tell him they're rayl quality :
wan a clargyman an' t'other a barrysthur,
an suddin bysiness over the wather."

" Holloa ! what's amiss," inquired the
master of the " Amber Wave," standing at
the cabin door of the dying bride.

" A clergyman and another individual
want to pay their expenses to New York,"
answered the mate.

" Heaven be thanked," thought the lady
inwardly, while Captain Nicholson exclaimed aloud,—

" If one is a minister I shall give both
a free voyage," softly muttering, " It
will be worth it and more to take this

contraband-looking marriage off my hands."

"Show up the passengers," he added, "and detain the boat, some one may go back in her."

The two new comers advanced with the obvious air and appearance of gentlemen, he of the white tie bowing to the captain, who remained outside the compartment, saying, " I thank you for your courtesy, allow me to introduce myself, the Rev. Randall Massey, of St. Werburgh's, Galway, and my friend, Mr. Fawcett, who accompanies me to America, on a mission of vital importance."

The answer of the commander of the " Amber Wave," was agreeably sufficient, as saluting the arrivals, he observed,—

" Gentlemen, you are welcome. Send the luggage on board."

" Captain, pray do not permit the boat

to return yet," entreated the invalid
earnestly from within the sick-chamber.

"That reminds me!" exclaimed her
auditor, starting eagerly, "you, sir,"
addressing the man of divinity, "have
arrived most opportunely to render a
signal service to me."

"Which I shall be very happy to do,"
was suavely replied, accompanied by a
grave depression of the head.

"Then you and your friend will please ·
to follow me into this berth," observed the
old mariner, leading the way to the hue-
less bride. "This young lady is danger-
ously ill, in fact, I fear past all hope of
recovery. Her betrothed is there standing
opposite, and he even now wishes to be
married, that thus in death they may join
hearts long fondly united in life."

"But—I—I cannot," responded the new
voyager in an alarmed voice.

"You will excuse my friend," promptly interposed the companion of the reverend gentleman, "but the situation is so novel he hardly comprehends it. However, he shall marry them;" adding in an undertone, " hesitate, and we are lost."

"Give me a moment's consideration," pleaded the clergyman, "you are all strangers, which perplexes me," and, leaning on his associate's arm, they left the cabin, returning, however, in an incredible short time, when the ceremony proceeded, *sans* the usual habiliments, unavoidable in the unwonted emergency.

The bride of death looked pale and wan, but composed to a wonderful degree. Her future spouse also appeared calm, but the celebrant suffered under some ungovernable mental influence, until at length, when the names of the contracting parties were given out as being respectively Fanny

Chalmers and Vincent Darecourt, he could proceed no further, but reeled back like a drunken idiot.

"My friend is unfortunately subject to attacks of hysteria," interposed the "barrysther," "but he as quickly recovers," whereupon whispering in his companion's ear,—

"Remember your wife; save her;" and certainly the stricken officiant recovered marvellously, when the marital rite continued to its close, the formal certificate stood signed "Fanny Chalmers, Vincent Darecourt, William Nicholson, the Rev. Randall Massey, and Arthur Fawcett."

As this document was tendered to the now married lady, she sat up immediately, and, clasping the clergyman's hand, wrung it with actual violence, saying,—

"Heaven bless you for this kindness," adding at once, "I feel so much better that

I shall undertake the journey to land with my dearest husband," and instantly springing from the bed, she stood up erect, ready dressed for the occasion.

Her consort sunk into a chair with abject terror, while the old sailor held on by the bunk, the minister and his friend rushing out in actual alarm.

A few moments afterwards the two latter were passed by the united pair, the gentleman pale and downcast, while that late seemingly dying girl looked well and confident, walking towards the boat amid the wonderment of their silent but astonished observers.

The Benedick had already taken his seat therein, and his wife was about to follow, when, on the top of the gangway, the clergyman impulsively sprang to her side, speaking in a low solemn voice, unheard by all except herself.

For an instant she swayed as if disposed to tumble into the sea, but in another her normal composure had returned, softly answering through her gleaming teeth,—

" Sir, I am the sole arbitress of my own actions."

The yawl was now rapidly rowed away from the vessel, and approached the bold headland, while every eye on board the " Amber Wave" was centred on the departing " Bride of the deep."

CHAPTER II.

AT last the speedy fly-boat moves from her berth at Broadstone, and under the influence of these two gaily clad juvenile jocks and the anti-Derbyite bony-looking horses they bestride, who are nevertheless good safe movers, away she goes, merrily laving in the sluggish waters of the Royal Canal, which flows through a magnificent richly wooded country, lying in calm, soft grandeur between Dublin and Longford— its extreme points at both ends. In the " Fly " the usual devilry, mirth, noise, and waste of time was indulged; but Lucy Darecourt sat on this night pensive and

reflective, beside her equally retiring companion O'Grady, wondering why they
could all seem so happy, if perhaps foolish,
while she grew heartily ill at the page
of trouble in her day-book of life—
which was only just opened and not even
read.

The Outlaw's thoughts were widely different; the one active consideration with
him being, are these easily influenced people
representative of their fellows, or are they
susceptible of that foundation of solid
discernment and self-control which alone
endows man with the free consciousness
of personal superiority? Remaining thus
fully absorbed and preoccupied, they
spoke not, but each felt that the scene
of jollification was deepening into one of
rancour and possible strife at the card-
table opposite, wherefrom high-sounding,
unusual words had been already heard,

which was the more surprising, two of
the players being ladies, opposed to whom
were four inflamed-looking members of the
opposite sex.

Several unavailing attempts had been
made to subdue the apprehended *émeute*
as the play proceeded and the deposits
became larger, but despite all counsel or
counter-admonition on it went, the gentlemen growing more flushed and heated,
while these two impassibly calm partners,
mother and daughter, uniquely transferred
the proceeds of each round into the elder
female's pocket; and although declining
to bet, no matter how insignificant an
amount, they were always ready to in-
crease the stakes, in every instance securing
the game.

The losers were not the only ones who
supposed that this extravagant run of
good luck must change; but no, they

kept on pitilessly winning, winning, winning.

There was another, however, who with
folded arms and a disdainful smile looked
keenly from a distance, freely imbibing all
that was passing—indeed, more than some
opined.

O'Grady growing weary of the discordant spectacle, said,—

"Mrs. Darecourt, will you remain or
accompany me outside for a stroll?"

"Thank you," she gently replied; "I
am safe here; besides I would like to see
who is victor in such an extraordinary
contest, which cannot endure much
longer."

"Then I shall seek the solitude of the
external world for a little," he observed, and
bowing left her.

Lucy Darecourt now became aware
that the stern, inflexible eyes of the con-

templative young man closely followed the figure of an old military-looking gentleman approaching her, who with perfect good grace assumed the seat just vacated by the Outlaw, but in her preoccupation of watching the game Lucy soon forgot such a trivial incident.

After continuing thus—how long she knew not—her attention was distracted by that grey-haired neighbour remarking,—

"Excuse me, miss, yet upon my word it is quite a feast for my eyes to note how earnestly you observe that never-ending system of winning."

Lucy blushed slightly while answering,—

"Indeed, sir, I have been regarding it as closely as the distance permits."

"May I inquire if you play the game?"

"Certainly not," spoken decisively; "nor could I even have believed ladies indulged in such a pastime."

" Ah, my good girl, you know very little of the inner lives of some who are looked up to and accepted as models in the best circles of society."

" I regret it," she observed, " as being unfeminine and questionable, although the novelty has chained me here against my better self for so long, and—I must now retire," rising.

But intuitively feeling that he was the cause of her leaving, the very gentle-manly old man bowed most politely, saying apologetically,—

" Pray overlook my unintended inter-ference," he smiled, " which your inte-rested manner betrayed me into so—*au revoir.*"

Finding that she was again alone, Lucy Darecourt resumed her chair just as it became evident that the climax between the suitors for the hand of fortune in that speculation and those who could not lose it had been reached.

"Damnation!" exclaimed one of the quartette, his last guinea exhausted, which these females had just added to their previous gains, "I'll wager my existence, it's a downright swindle."

The lady gamesters sat erect and unconcerned, although the subject of such dreadful suspicion, it being the opinion of more than their opponents that it was very anomalous how they continued to win indefinitely.

The stolid, contemptuous indifference wherewith the losers were regarded by the successful pair now leaving the table, maddened the one who had already spoken and who now thundered,—

"I'll have my honest money back, you double-dyed swindlers!"

"Hear! hear!" approvingly followed

from the other three victims and a few zealous sympathizers.

There was now no visible means of escape for Lucy, who became greatly alarmed, all the doors being blocked by eager spectators both from within and without; whereupon, believing that the disturbance would bring back her protector, she resumed her late position nervously awaiting his return.

The elder of the two accused females drew herself up imperiously, and looking scornfully around inquired,—

"Is there no one here who will protect us ladies from vulgar insult by low-bred, insignificant brawlers?"

On which the very gentlemanly looking military old man stepped forth with alacrity, observing,—

"Madam, allow me to assist you in this deplorable misunderstanding."

"We want our money; we'll not be robbed," was hoarsely retorted.

"Accord me a moment's patience," pleaded the mediator, "and I will endeavour to unravel the mistake."

"Are you anything to them?" suspiciously demanded.

"I have not had the pleasure of seeing these ladies before," he answered with a gesture and tone indignantly repelling the doubt implied in the question.

"Then listen to the gentleman," urged several voices, the justice of which advice was admitted by all.

At this moment the possessed, thoughtful stranger, whom Lucy had observed watching the very gentlemanly military old man, now advanced cautiously to where she still sat, and in a whisper said,—

"Be guarded; see that you have lost nothing," and passed onwards.

For an instant the young girl mused upon
these odd words, but almost as soon she
reflected, "He was speaking to himself,
and not to me, or he would have remained
to explain; but how I wish Mr. O'Grady
were here."

"You undertook to play the game?"
continued the benign intermediary.

"Yes, but not to be cheated," one
wrathfully attested.

"That is not just," proceeded the peace-
maker; "fortune cannot be controlled,
and the idea is impossible that you could
or would be unfairly deprived of your
money."

"No more of this mystification—we'll
have it back! we'll have it back!" was
jointly shouted.

Hereupon Lucy felt greatly frightened,
starting to her feet, when, oh, great
heavens! the papers for Vincent were

gone. Wild and maddened she put her
hands to her temples, the momentous
words of the stranger flashing upon her
in all their gravity—"Be guarded; see
that you have lost nothing."

"Where is he now? Oh how can I tell
him?" she asked herself, while there in the
distance, remote from every one, but still
intently discounting all that was passing,
he confidently stood.

Lucy was speedily beside him, when,
anticipating her errand, he asked,—

"What is missing?

"Oh, sir," she answered vehemently,
"the very ransom of my husband."

"What? one so young to speak of the
ransom of a husband," was echoed in
kind, subdued words.

"Alas, it is even so, sir, and my whole
prospect of happiness is centred in the
recovery of those stolen papers."

"I sincerely sympathize with you, and will help to regain the property if it be possible."

"But you can assist me, else why speak these kind words of caution?" the interesting applicant looked pleadingly into his face.

"My assistance is at your service, and I cautioned you because I knew of the necessity for doing so. Pray resume your chair, and depend on my aid."

As Lucy turned, going back to her late station, the stranger inquired,—

"May I ask if the parcel is open or sealed?"

"Sealed."

"That is lucky, no enclosures can have yet been abstracted. One word more, did it bear any superscription?"

"Yes, it was addressed ' *For the Honble. Vincent Darecourt.*"

She stopped abruptly, turning colourless, murmuring in broken accents,—

" I have betrayed my husband."

But the unknown gentleman had already grasped her hands, his countenance beaming with much joyful surprise as he proceeded,—

" What ! Mrs. Darecourt are you the wife of my old friend. Vincent, son and heir of Lord Darecourt ? "

" Yes."

" A singular circumstance indeed ; married to him, whom I have not met for years. But we will talk it over by-and-by. Be content, you shall have the papers and one very influential hand to aid in all that can benefit yourself and your husband."

Ere recovering from her astonishment, he retired, saying,—

" Do not leave the seat until I come to you."

By the time Lucy regained her position the climax in the scene of discord had been reached, while the fly-boat was being guided into the usual halting-place.

Retreating before their irate aggrieved opponents, the mother and daughter gamesters slowly but surely approach to where Lucy Darecourt was seated ; there being brought to bay, having reached the limit of the saloon, its last window standing exactly above her chair.

The threats and looks of violence became insupportable, although the very gentlemanly military old man still ‘kept between the rival parties, but nature had grown infirm in the parent, who at last feebly uttered,—

" I have not one penny ; you can search me."

A fiery yell of baffled execration followed this announcement, the quarto of defeated players rushing at the now trembling exhausted female, bending low behind Lucy, and one of these implacable antagonists had actually raised his hand as though to strike at the prostrate form, when, like the whiz from a cannon shot, the casement was burst through over her head, and the four belligerent gamblers lay stretched upon the floor, while the Outlaw exclaimed,—

"Down, mongrels of men that would dare to assail a woman!"

But, alas, the picket, who had pursued him when the fly-boat touched the low jetty, already formed around, encompassing the avenger on every side, whereupon the very gentlemanly military old man in a harsh, biting tone of triumph screamed,—

"Soldiers, give no quarter! arrest the notorious O——"

"Hold, Colonel B——!" vociferated the

strange unknown friend of Lucy's husband, who now, as promised, stood by her side, and whom she had besought to save O'Grady's life. "We have met before," the interrupter continued, "and I demand the liberation of this lady's companion," pointing to Lucy, "the restoration of the documents purloined from her, and the money which these two persons," indicating the female gamesters, "have falsely acquired at cards."

Both mother and daughter looked piteous in their degraded state, while the very gentlemanly military old man tottered to the side of the young dictator, muttering, "Grant me a moment in private," and wonderingly all beheld the pair retire out of hearing. Even the Outlaw appeared interested in the odd proceeding.

"Oh! spare us for the sake of our child," pleaded the very gentlemanly old man.

" This time I will, but on the next occasion I shall expose you and them at every hazard.   Remember our last meeting in the Rue Saint Thomas du Louvre.   I saved you then under a promise to abandon this career of swindling, although but now I watched you, while standing behind the chairs of your dupes, signify to your wife and daughter the cards to play."

" The money and papers will be returned, but do not persist in the surrender of the renowned prisoner.   Five hundred guineas are offered for his—"

" Stay," was interrupted; " I know nothing whatever of him, I have promised that he shall be free, and my word must be redeemed."

They now returned to the anxious crowd, when the very gentlemanly old man, in broken accents, said,—

" Soldiers, shoulder arms and march to

your quarters; there is a grievous mistake. Here are the papers, madam," delivering to Lucy Darecourt the prized documents. " This is the proceeds of the card-playing," taking the money from his pocket, and placing it on the table. One alone noticed how dexterously the specie had been passed from wife to husband. " You, sir," turning to O'Grady, "are free, and I deeply apologize for the unwitting error of arresting you for another," accompanied by a profound salute, "knowing what I now do from this gentleman, Sir Mervyn Mervyn," indicating Lucy's new friend.

" Sir Mervyn devil!" muttered the chagrined retiring picket, biting their lips. " The Colonel and his precious lot have been up to their old tricks. Through it he lost the post of Aide-de-camp to the Lord-Lieutenant, and now he has saved the Outlaw!"

CHAPTER III.

SOCIETY was not unprepared to hear of the
demise of the noble owner of Darecourt,
nor of his having declared by last will
and testament that so far as he could,
he had disinherited his son Vincent in
favour of his nephew Dorrington, who was
to succeed him in the title of Lord of Darecourt and all in the present or future appertaining thereunto, relying on the Government, of which he had been a loyal
and consistent follower, to support this
nephew Dorrington's right to the aforesaid
title and possessions against the machinations or devices of the previously-mentioned

Vincent, who, by rebellious acts and asso-
ciations had forfeited the parental affection as well as the protection of the laws
of the realm.

The foregoing formed the gist of the
authoritative pronouncement put forth to
the world on the day of the old patrician's
death, attested as appeared on the original
document by Brien Flynn, and Robert
Arkwright, Esquires.

One section of the community thought
the deceased stood a bad chance of being
himself forgiven when he had thus denied
this clemency to an only son, but on the
other side it was held that the father had
performed a public duty in cutting off a
disloyal, unnatural offspring.

Brien Flynn, Esq., sat composedly in
the carved oak chair lately occupied by
Lord Darecourt, whose earthly remains
were overhead, waiting their last full-dress

sepulture. He had carefully locked the edge-stuffed door and drawn the hand-sewn ornamental screen thereto, the more effectually to prevent the possibility of the existence of any aperture through which an eye might observe his search in each drawer or recess, whose contents were added to the heap of miscellanea now confronting him. Dexterously he put aside that which a hasty glance satisfied him could not be of import to the cause wherein he laboured, and it seemed astonishing with what precision this resolution was arrived at, having regard to the fact that he could hardly cipher, and that whatever he did know was the result of a strong natural habit of perseverance.

After a couple of hours exhausted in the process of exploration, he carefully separated all the materials relevant from his point of view, the remainder being returned to their former positions with a marked degree of exactitude.

Then he proceeded to subdivide those which he had selected, and very soon they were formed into two separate parcels, one of which was consigned to his outer coat, the other still remaining on the table.

" Ha! ha !" mused the industrious middleman, evidently pleased with the result of his labour, "this I can use or not, at will " (indicating the parcel still in view), " bud the other wan in the overcoat 'ill giv me enof av money to hide wheniver I like, or whoiver gits the property, for some time; I think Dorrington's losth; indayde id wudn't throuble me aytherway wor id not for Miss Chalmers, and I can't belayve she'd cut her sthick out av this world till she'd left her mark behind somehow or other. Iths all playne now, the ould lord's

gon, Vincent darn't show his nose, an'
Dorrington has the coasth clear be mayn's
av mesel' an Arkwright—though Arkwright can't be found nowhere for love or
money—Sir Marvyn book'd him the noight
he kem an us togither, an' he warn't seen
since; av coorse I don't say all I think
about his absince, the sowldiers may tell
lies av they plaze, bud mesel' suspicts he's
gon afther his wife, more fool for that
sayme; I saw he wor a wake kind av a
craythur, an' that's me opinyan anyhow.

"What a nice thing to put yoursel' down
Brien Flynn, Esquire, in the dockiemint all
the world knows av be this, or soon will,
which is the sayme; Brien Flynn (he
echoed with a laugh) an esquire too, ha, ha,
ha! I cudn't hav don more av Dorrington
wor here, nothin like purcishun," was
mentally continued, "id ill shut up any
hopes av Misther Vincent or his wife, for

the rayson the govermint are axed to lind a hilpin hand, an' be the sayme sthroke 'twill bring Dorrington home agin where-iver he is, an make him very much obleeged to me in throth. Shuppoze they wint down at say, what thin (he proceeded) who's to git the property? be Jabers 'tis an the cards afore the gaym's pled out I may be the lord—not the lord I mayne bud hould the hard land, for shure be the sayme pin as writ the false will an tistamint, layvin id to Dorrington, cudn't I layve id to mesel'." Elongating his legs and sitting in an erect posture, he complaisantly surveyed himself as he thought, " The idee's in me hed I'd look a very daycint Lord Darecoort, an' av id coms to that I'll not be backward in goin' forward, an' why not to be shure?" He paused a moment, biting his nails, then renewed the train of pleasant cogitation. " I hav the chist hayp'd wid goold, bud I

think I'll git id away somehow afore Dorrington turns up, in case av daynger.
Another thing, av I am forced to purclaim
mysel' the rayl lord, an' I'd thry id av
nicessary (the brows grew heavily dark,
while his lips locked in each other),
what's thim all to me, how do I know
what they'll do av I giv thim the chance?
No, Dorrington, av ye do return ye'll
foind I'm not so much yer tool as ye
think; an' av ye don't com' back, be all
that's saycrid, I'll sthamp me foot an the
ground in Darecoort an call it me own;
who can privint me, av the ould man over-
hed doesn't git up to deny his handwritin,
which isn't probable? (smiling facetiously),
an' wont the long purse in coorse av time
do the rest at Dublin Castle for the toitle.
At all evints I'll thry, shure the toss av a
tin-pinny piece 'ill ind id wan way or
tother."

A sharp reverberating knock now rudely upset his line of reasoning, and the pleasurable exalted position into which he had gradually worked himself in the glow of a fervid imagination, was roughly assailed as a second summons followed in a louder and more decided manner, at the same instant the handle of the lock being vigorously turned and returned.

" Let me in at once," ordered a female voice from the outside.

" Who are you ? " inquired the deputy anxiously, undoing the bolt.

" Lady Darecourt," firmly spoken, and before he could realize the stirring words the door was shot open by Fanny Chalmers, who passed him, walking straight to the seat he had just vacated, and placing her hand upon the documents so sedulously arranged, she confronted Flynn, sharply exclaiming,—

" " This is not the agent's department."

" Oh heaven, Miss—"

" Lady Darecourt in future, please," was
borne to his astounded ears with such a
cold possessed enunciation and manner, that
the listener dropped into a seat, his breath
coming quickly while his heart beat faster.
The occupant of the carved oak chair was
now actively perusing the several papers
contained in that angular parcel, to all
appearances oblivious of the wondering
eyes of Brien Flynn, who, undecided which
way to turn or what to do, grew wholly
beside himself, as in a meek timid voice he
inquired,—

" Are you married, mam ? "

The possessor of the favourite seat of
the late Lord Darecourt jumped to her
feet, and in another trice stood beside the
cowering questioner, whom she held rigidly
by the coat collar, her fierce relentless eyes

seeking out his, but he felt unable to upraise an averted face, the weight and superiority of that determined woman having already conquered, and well did he realize this signal overthrow ere she hissed into his ear,—

"Do you mean to insult me, or shall I send for my husband, and ask his lordship to cast you out of doors as a base hireling who forgets the respect due to his noble employers?"

"Forgiv me, bud id is so suddin', miss."

"Your ladyship," was authoritatively dictated.

"Yer leddyship av coorse," he replied hastily, as though it were a great relief to get the reluctant words from off his unwilling tongue.

She appeared mollified, and, returning to her previous position, in a relaxed, somewhat softened voice, suggested,—

"Probably you did not measure the relevancy of your incautious words, Flynn?"

"I did not, yer—"

"Ladyship," she interposed haughtily, adding, "you now know the form of recognition demanded by my position as Lady Darecourt; let there be no further necessity for having to remind you of your duty."

"I am obleeged to yer leddyship, an' in futhur I'll be an me bist manners."

"In which event we can get on very well, but not otherwise, now we understand each other," followed by a significant inclination of the head.

"I'll be as good as me word yer leddyship 'll hav no furth'r cauze to riprimand me."

"What do these papers refer to?" was the short pointed inquiry, motioning towards the documents lying on the table.

The agent winced under her searching glance, as he furtively replied,—

" To the property, yer leddyship."

" But you took them from out these drawers ? " indicating the different recesses before her.

" I did, yer leddyship."

" And this was the late Lord Darecourt's library."

" Id wor, yer leddyship ; bud I don all me bysiness wid his lordship here."

" Surely you did not examine his private communications ? "

" No, yer leddyship."

" How is it, then, that I find you in possession of these personal belongings which are all marked private ? "

Brien Flynn felt struck dumb by the question and the scathing look of its author.

" Is there no answer ? "

" Well, yer leddyship, I—I—"

" Go on, please."

" I thought id me dhuty to look afther the affairs av the lasth an' prisint Lord Darecoort."

" Was it your duty to abstract these several papers ? "

" What, yer leddyship ? " aghast.

" To pilfer from private relics of the Darecourt family ? "

" Oh, murther an' ouns, yer leddyship doesn't mayne that I'm a robber ! " half screamed the agent, rising in his seat.

" That is exactly what I do mean and more," mercilessly retorted.

" What, yer leddyship?" he faltered completely overcome.

" That you have already stolen other writings than these, and of greater value."

" Oh Lord! oh Lord!" was whined piteously; " don't wrong me intirely— don't, shure I'm innishunt."

Unmindful of which she ruthlessly continued,—

" How long is the late Lord Darecourt dead ? "

" A few hours, yer leddyship."

"Were you in the Castle when he expired ? "

" Yis, yer leddyship."

" I suppose you attended to his individual necessities before leaving the deceased nobleman ? "

" I did, yer leddyship."

" Thence I presume you came direct to the library ? "

" I did, yer leddyship."

" And you have remained here since ? "

" Yis, yer leddyship."

" Then the missing documents are in this room ? ay, and in your possession; no prevarication," she loftily added, " bring them to me."

"Oh dear, oh dear," he feebly exclaimed, mechanically moving to his overcoat. "are ye a human bein' who can turn me inside out as ye plaze?"

"I am a human being, and I can be humane as well; but I shall trample on every one who dares to oppose me," she continued without looking towards him. "In a parchment, No. 137, now in your coat, is a draft on Lord Darecourt's bankers, payable to bearer, for five thousand guineas."

Petrified he gazed vacantly at her, bereft of power to speak or move.

Unheeding, however, she proceeded,—

"Your intention was to convert this warrant into gold at the first opportunity, and add it to your other very large gains."

"Don't, for pity sake, yer leddyship," and groaning, he fell upon his knees before her, wailing and wringing his hands, as he intreated, "Only giv me time, I'll open me whole heart to ye, for shure iverything ye say is thrue."

A broad smile of unconcealed triumph still lingered upon her composed face, as taking the folded bundle from him, she said languidly,—

"Resume your seat, Flynn; I shall become even your friend, upon certain conditions."

Rapidly and carefully she compared each of the numbered papers contained in this parcel, with the comprehensive tabulated register before her, the latter not being understood by the agent, although containing the information whereby she had so completely surprised him, and having satisfied herself that all were restored to their original places, she locked each recess separately, and afterwards the outer door of the ponderous cabinet, putting the keys in her pocket.

Brien Flynn sat thinking what would he not give to escape from before her scrutinizing glance, or that he had Dorrington Darecourt to cope with, but,— "'Tis ividint she masthers him as she did me," he pondered; "so av coorse she knows iverything."

Wheeling round in her roomy chair she now centres all the energy of her eyes and facial expression into one imperious look of extreme depth and cautiousness, slowly inquiring,—

"You have not known my husband long ?"

"Ye mayne Misther—? "

"I mean the present Lord Darecourt."

"I beg yer leddyship's pardon, av coorse id is me Lord Darecoort. I hav not

known him virry long, bud hasn't his lordship tould ye iverything?"

Not deigning to notice the question
she went on,—

"You were aware that Lord Darecourt's
only child was Mr. Vincent?"

"Yis, yer leddyship."

"Why did you tell me that Mr. Dorrington was this son of Lord Darecourt?"

"I thought he—"

"Avoid dissimulation; I will permit no
trifling with truth, sir."

The intended falsehood became choked
in the deputy's throat, who suppliantly
responded,—

"I'll tell ye openly, yer leddyship,
bekayze I must do so, we intinded to
desayv yer leddyship."

"Both of you?"

"No not at first. I stharted id, an'

aftherwards Misther Dorrington followed id up."

" What was your object, Flynn ? "

"Must I sphake playnly, yer leddyship?"

" That is what I desire, sir."

" Thin I tould Misther Dorrington as how ye wor the virry wan to make the futhur Leddy Darecoort."

A pause ensued, but assuredly the girl did not look displeased at what had just been stated.

" Mr. Dorrington was Lord Darecourt's nephew," she observed somewhat abstractedly.

" He wor, yer leddyship ; bud hasn't his lordship tould ye all this afore ? "

Again she unheeded the inquiry.

" Flynn, have you any doubt that Mr. Vincent is gone for ever ? "

" None, yer leddyship."

" May he not return ? "

" Av he did he'd be thrown into prizin, I've phrovided for all that."

" You ?"

" Twor me yer leddyship."

" But his wife is not a likely person to surrender, besides she has large means wherewith to prosecute their pretensions."

" Ah, that I've also turn'd upside down," he exclaimed jubilantly.

" How ?"

" Be gittin' the govermint to sayquesthrate all her fortin' as belongin' to her husband."

To the Darecourt agent's amazement " her leddyship" proffered her hand, and seeing his dubiety in returning the salutation she vigorously clasped his, holding it firmly while bringing her face close to him, demanding, " On the peril of your life speak out, is my husband Lord Darecourt's nephew ?"

Astonishment was depicted in Flynn's every lineament while muttering,—

" Hasn't his lordship tould yer ?"

" Answer my question at once, sir."

" Thin he is Lord Darecoort's nephey, yer leddyship," he replied with downcast eyes.

" You and my husband are the cause of Mr. Vincent Darecourt's banishment ?"

" Hasn't his lordship tould ye ?"

" Yes or no, sir ?"

" Yis, we got him arristid, an' afther he eskayped."

She rose still holding his hand—he also got up—and with each syllable deeply accentuated, inquired in a laboured voice, " Did the late Lord Darecourt really disinherit Vincent, an only child, and appoint his cousin, Dorrington, successor to the title and estates of Darecourt ?"

" Hasn't his lordship tould— "

" Go on, sir; no hesitation with me."

" He did not, yer leddyship."

" Then the public announcement en-
dorsed by you and another, named Arkwright, is part of this prearranged fraud ?"

" Id is, yer leddyship, bud hasn't his
lordship tould— "

" Peace, peace," she uttered with a
gesture of impatience, adding, " my husband and you have mutually concerted
and carried out this dishonest scheme so
far with success."

" We hav, yer leddyship; bud hasn't his
lordship tould ye all himsel' ?"

" He has told me nothing," she replied
with great emphasis and precision, resuming her chair.

" Thin, yer leddyship, thinkin' as how ye
knew iverything, I wor the first to let the
cat out av the bag: oh dear ! oh dear ! oh
dear ! "

"You alone have been my informant," "her leddyship" uttered in an absent-minded, listless tone.

"Oh, wurra, wurra, what 'ill be don now, what 'ill be don?" Flynn sorrowfully entreated by word and look, when passionately starting upwards, his counterfeit mistress exclaimed aloud,—

"Despite my husband and you, ay even heaven and earth, I shall remain the noble Lady of Darecourt." She quickly swept out of the library, the stupified agent falling forward on the table.

CHAPTER IV.

THE private coach-and-four waiting the arrival of Sir Mervyn Mervyn, to take him to his large estates near Roscommon, also carried the Hon. Mrs. Darecourt and the renowned O'Grady.

"It is on the road, and I claim the right, as an old friend of your husband, to insist on the acceptance of my hospitality: besides," added the baronet, " in a strange place, away from friends, and one at least," indicating the patriot, "eagerly sought for, will it not best advance the mission both are pursuing, by allowing me to associate with you in rescuing Vincent Darecourt?"

This friendly advice was so patent, and the influence of Sir Mervyn Mervyn of such moment, that in a very short time the travellers were, as we have already stated, occupants of the massive vehicle conveying him to his inheritance, which he had never yet seen. Triumphal arches, wide spreading flags, bonfires composed of large barrels, turf and fir-trees (principally abstracted from his own enclosures), welcomed the new landlord. What cruel satire did not this word " new " imply to those living upon that property, the young baronet being indeed a stranger, as had been his fathers before him, though these broad acres had grown old in the ownership and possession of the Mervyn family. Is not the curse of non-residence a deadly blight, imbuing the country with fraud ? and will not Ireland ever remain an easy prey to the adventurous hireling of those who neither look for themselves, nor can be seen by the tillers of the land?

The fatted calf was of course roasted on the lawn facing the " big house," where the good things of life were liberally bestowed and as freely partaken of; from far and near coming throngs all united in evincing the warmest, most genuine feeling of respect towards Sir Mervyn Mervyn. The cards of the leading families in the adjacent counties were there in galore, and on a day yet to be named, the popular landlord was to receive deputations from those representative of the middle classes. To-night, however, he desired to be in private, and pleasantly the time ebbed away in the agreeable society of those new acquaintances, Mrs. Darecourt and O'Grady.

Insensibly the conversation turned on the latter, of whom their host had heard a great deal, but never other than in connexion with his public, daring exploits. Lucy also became anxious to know what had led to his overtly taking up arms in rebellion.

Their auditor was not in a mood to discourse, nor yet did he wish to deny the natural longing of those importuning him to the recital.

"Explain its immediate cause," urged the baronet, "I ask no more, for surely, some original distinctive act will be recollected by you as that which precipitated the step."

"There was a circumstance that more than all else made me what I am."

"Oh, do tell it," pleaded Lucy, supplemented by their host's volunteered promise that they would ask nothing further.

Then replied the Outlaw firmly and measuredly, "You, Sir Mervyn Mervyn, above all others, are the cause of my various attempts, baffled though they have been in pursuit of my country's freedom."

" A stupendous hallucination, considering we never met before, and that at the period you allude to I had not even thought of visiting Ireland. What a capital joke, Mrs. Darecourt," added the young man; "do you not think so? ha, ha!" and he laughed heartily.

Lucy, however, did not join in the one-sided merriment; something in that iron, thoughtful brow of the patriot forbidding it, who waited the evanescence of the genuine mirth, when he pointedly reiterated,—

" I repeat, Sir Mervyn, you are the cause of my public career, as identified with opposition to the Government."

The lady felt embarrassed at the colour mounting to the baronet's face, who, nevertheless, quickly controlled himself, saying, in a light, somewhat uncertain tone,—

" I will not longer press a point on which you are so decided, although I gave my reason for asserting its impracticability, not being in Ireland at the time the incident, whatever it may be, occurred."

" I know you were not," was very quickly replied.

" Then how can it be possible that I have influenced you in any way directly or indirectly ? "

"Sir Mervyn Mervyn," began the Outlaw, " judge for yourself ; " and with a voice of irresistible pathos he told the Dangan eviction as we read of it in the beginning. Omitting nothing, and adding nothing, the harrowing narrative was impartially re-cited, and, influenced by the appearance of these sympathetic auditors, he went on *pari passu*, until, with a tenderness surprising in one currently associated with acts of intrepidity and courage, widely known and marvelled at, he came to the close, adding, "You have heard more from me than I would care to speak again, for the mien of the woman ought to be foreign to him compelled to checkmate life, with the world on the alert, crouching to expedite his exit therefrom."

"I am interested beyond measure in what you have related," exclaimed their attentive host, extending his arm across the table, "and I shall scrupulously atone for my unwitting neglect of duty, whereby such cruel wrongs were made possible, if not even fostered from the conviction of being perpetrated with impunity. Mr. Arkwright, the author of this unnatural scandal I have already summarily dismissed and sent away."

"I know where he is, and the secret is

mine alone," interposed the Outlaw with quiet assurance.

"I understood he went to rejoin his wife in England," observed Arkwright's late employer.

"That is not so," was decisively spoken.

"Where is he, Mr. O'Grady?" inquired Lucy Darecourt with a look of interest.

"An inmate of the deep vaults at Wentworth Abbey."

"Oh," she exclaimed mournfully, uplifting her hands, "it is a lamentable end."

"No," answered his captor, "the varlet will not perish although richly deserving it. He treacherously surrounded me with an escort of fifty picked troops, and while I stood waiting death from the guns already aimed at my breast, the cupidity of the wretch proved his downfall; not wishing to sacrifice the reward of five hundred guineas, which the Government

will gratefully pay for my arrest—
you see I am deserving of consideration,"
smiling—" he suggested terms of surrender, retiring into the ruins to privately
arrange them, when perforce he accepted
my conditions, for, touching a secret
spring, I precipitated us both into the
passage beneath."

"I would have mortally crushed the
worthless *canaille*," interrupted the baronet
with passionate emotion. "He fully me-
rited it, but, remembering my promise
to his good wife, I spared him, with
a warning against attempting to escape
before the elapse of three days, when
he would be at liberty to depart, instructing him how to find an exit from
the vault."

"Do you think he will ever forego this
unnatural resentment to you?" Lucy
asked.

"It is a difficult question to answer; however I have some hope of him, because that he so often spoke affectionately of Mrs. Arkwright. Were he to join her he might reform, indeed his somewhat remarkable utterance on my leaving was, remember in the day of peril to the true Darecourts I shall be your friend and theirs."

"Oh," she exclaimed with joyful fervour, "he may yet atone for much if not all of his misdeeds."

"Let him endeavour to do so, and I will aid in the good undertaking; but you, Mr. O'Grady must henceforth become my thought night and day, how to undo the past, restoring you to that society which you were made to adorn. English though I am, I cannot doubt that natures such as thine ought never to be placed unprepared face to face with seeming wrong, for like all that is generous and noble you yearn to share the cause wherein yourself is sacrificed."

The baronet was very hot as he finished, while the subject of his eulogy composedly observed,—

"It is not in the power of man to turn me from the conviction that in the end I will perish, because I can never recognize the oppressors of Ireland."

Ere the subject could be further proceeded with an announcement was made that the tenantry and others at the *fête* were anxiously awaiting the promised visit of the baronet previous to the close of the enjoyable entertainment.

"It has escaped my memory altogether, I will go at once," replied Sir Mervyn Mervyn, presenting his arm to Lucy. "Come, Mrs. Darecourt," he said, " do not deny me the pleasure of contributing to the gratification of others; besides, it will enliven you a little."

"Very many thanks," she answered softly. "I would rather remain and occupy myself in reading until you both return."

The Outlaw already liked the frank Englishman, and wishing also to afford his charge some amusement he urged her to go with them, ultimately succeeding in his persuasions.

Shortly afterwards the rich landlord, escorting that pale, handsome, melancholy-looking girl—many suggested she would be their future mistress—went through the respectful standing crowd, on whom the face and towering form of O'Grady made a visible impression.

At the further end of the draped temporary structure Sir Mervyn Mervyn stood acknowledging the welcoming congratulations of the large assembly, while for a long time his companion had not felt so well or happy; indeed it appeared as though the light-hearted Lucy Neville of the past was herself again.

The Outlaw too looked unusually interested, as with arms folded on his powerful breast he silently surveyed the pleasurable prospect, but beyond all was the new landlord charmed with the harmonious scene. Surely, he thought, such people as these ought not to be discarded. No, I will recognize our mutual obligations, and my countrymen shall learn that the Irish only want the justice of being truly understood by and of knowing those whom right and circumstances have placed over them to become the happiest, most contented race on earth.

At this instant the young wife started violently, holding the baronet's arm with a visible tremor, while looking towards the window on her left, from whence, almost at the same time, a sealed letter addressed to the Honourable Mrs. Vincent Darecourt was thrown, falling at her feet.

"I hope you are not ill?" he gently said, handing her the large missive.

"No, thank you, Sir Mervyn," tearing it distractedly open, as the colour returned to her agitated face.

A wild scream now smote that festive gathering, like a pall of the dead, covering and hiding their busy mirth.

Hushed and speechless all eyes are directed to where the landlord, Sir Mervyn Mervyn, stands tenderly supporting the fainting beautiful creature in his arms, her head inertly reclining against his breast, while the Outlaw in a solemn, deep voice, breathes the purport of that fated communication into his attentive ear :—

" My darling, beloved Wife,—One chance alone remains of safety. The soldiers are on our track. That ship in the offing will receive us on board, or we perish. I am broken-hearted. Pray for your unhappy

" Vincent."

———

The " Darecourt Arms " was largely attended on the occasion which we now wish to present to our reader, the landlord reigning supreme in the realms of good whisky and twisted hard Limerick tobacco.

The well-remembered chair of the old soldier, now no more, was still in its proud position of honoured loneliness, none daring to intrude upon its occupation since the Outlaw graced it at first, to their indignant surprise; but, ah, how welcome was he when recognized, and have they not often heartily desired to see him sit in it again, ay, go where he would, mid sunshine or darkness, their allegiance was loyally and voluntarily his.

The Widdy Flanagan, God bless her, she lingers in her usual free and easy posture; Cup-o'-Tay too leers from out his ordinary corner. There also is Tom, and there he will remain so long as the gate of time is open, and he can shoot its bolt at will.

" A tumbler of hot brandy for heaven's sake," entreated a human voice as, to the surprise of all the assembled company, a figure tottered into the room and sank on a chair. " Quick, I am faint, dying."

"Holy murther, 'tis Misther Arkwright," exclaimed the wondering crowd, surrounding the latest arrival.

Gulping the ardent spirits, the prostrate man cried out, " Bring me to the fire, I am cold, oh, so very cold," and he closed his weary eyes.

"Why we heerd he wor killed be the Outlaw," uttered several softly, pointing to the well-known agent, who seemingly slumbered; but starting in his chair, the emaciated form, with a great effort, articulated,—

"The noble O'Grady spared my life; if I survive, I shall atone for the wrongs I have inflicted on him and others." Whereupon the attenuated speaker became insensible.

CHAPTER V.

WE must now direct the attention of the reader to the opening pages of this work, which will carry us forward a period of about twelve years since the occurrences related in the last chapters took place. On the leading *dramatis personæ* incidental to our story, the incursion of time even for a dozen brief years was recorded in many ways which we shall notice by-and-by; but we must first revert to the once-known Dorrington Darecourt and Fanny Chalmers, now accredited Lord and Lady Darecourt, and to the only child of their shipwrecked marriage—a boy—another Dorrington of course, although in appearance he gravitated most to the maternal side, having a fair complexion, with a long face, while his father had developed into a loose, corpulent being, lazy in look and speech, but very amenable to his wife. Her ladyship had grown even thinner than of yore, the cheek-bones becoming more prominent, though the eyes receded deeper in their little sockets; yet her resolve to be the imperious arbiter of each and all with whom she came in contact was vividly reflected from that possessed, erect carriage, scrutinizing glance, and laboured hauteur imported into every gesture and utterance.

Dorrington junior, as we have just observed, resembled his mother, but not in that iron will and supple frame; nay, therein he was unlike her, being delicate and effeminate in appearance, while in manner he looked shy and retiring.

But what of Brien Flynn, factotum in, of, and for all relating to the Darecourt property; yes, he too had changed by the influx of time, becoming bent in figure and worn in face, while the acquisition of green spectacles more than all else seemingly qualified him for his onerous duties as the "grinder," the scornful epithet now popularly applied to him. If being infallible in never delaying an instant in demanding payment of that which was but then due; in deferring payment even for a single hour upon any conceivable pretext whatever, while always refusing to liquidate his own debts unless driven to do so, formed a qualification for the responsible post of agent, it must be conceded that he was perfection. Under this inflexible sway the spirit of manhood was fairly hammered out of the tenantry.

Lord Darecourt had long ceased to

exercise any personal control in the manage-
ment of the property, leaving it wholly in
the hands of his wife and deputy. This
pair mutually distrusted each other; but,
withal, maintained a careful, practical ap-
preciation of the rights and convention-
alities due to their respective positions,
thereby avoiding the possibility of colliding
upon any one point, while the superiority
and discipline of her " Leddyship " pressed
upon Flynn like a huge incubus, wherefrom he only found relief by inwardly con-
fessing " she rules the roost," and it is no
ordinary personal sacrifice to feel and
admit we are beaten. The occasion of
which we are now writing proved an
eventful and stirring one for the possessors
of Darecourt. Breakfast lay untasted between the careless lord and his consort, and
the petted, hitherto licensed boy had been
relegated to the nursery with an imperious

mandate—" I shall not allow Master Dorrington down to-day again, I am worried ;"
this first instance of rejection by his
mamma making an indelible impression
on its dual recipient, son and nurse.

Dorrington senior continued to stare
vacantly at the unsipped coffee, while his
wife rose hastily from the table, and
paced the room, exclaiming,—

" What can detain the agent ? "

" You ought not to be so impatient, my
dear, he has never waited upon us at
this hour before, and is probably dressing
to answer your summons."

" People like him should always be
ready for their superiors," she snappishly
retorted, resuming her reproachful look
and brisk walk.

After a short interval the acquiescent
Brien Flynn bowed himself in, and
cringingly saluting his noble employers,

became seated in the chair indicated by her ladyship, with a seemly inquiry as to their respective health, and an earnest hope that nothing had occurred of an unusual nature to cause his having been sent for.

"It is of an unusual nature," answered Lady Darecourt; "judge for yourself, Flynn," she added, pushing a large, folded document bearing an official stamp towards him.

Resting his green spectacles on the sharp ridge of his nose, between those ferret-like eyes, the middleman took up the formal paper, which he almost immediately relinquished with a white or rather a whitish-green expression upon his disturbed face, observing mechanically—

"She's gon' afore the shuparyor Judges, claimin' the estates av Darecoort as the widdy av Misther Vincent, who's dead an' berry'd."

"Which you are not certain of," rejoined his restless mistress, "and it is of little consequence compared with the fact that she has already gained the former solicitors of the Darecourt family to espouse her cause."

"That's sarious, anyhow, bud can I ax how does yer leddyship com to know av this?"

"You are not always accurate, sir, whilst I try never to omit anything; look at the citation again, and you will see that the legal agents to the suit are those of the late Lord Darecourt, with all their private knowledge of the family to help her petition."

"Yer leddyship's sagacity is wondher-ful," responded the deputy; "an' I beg pardon for overlookin' the important news ;" he inwardly added, " that's how ye hav me at yer feet, for shure the divil cudn't put ye out av yer latithude in anythin'."

While her husband looked supine and indolent, Lady Darecourt was bristling with vigour and ingenuity, thinking how best to meet and conquer in the proximate struggle.

In a diffident manner, appreciable in one who felt he was dealing with his superior, Brien Flynn, unmindful of Lord Darecourt, addressed his wife, saying,—

" I'd like to know av yer leddyship has any sittled kind av an idaya what is bist to be don ? "

" You generally find me possessed of an idea," was answered tartly.

" That I do, yer leddyship."

" Yes, and I have one now which admits of no hesitation."

" What is id, yer leddyship ? "

"Get Vincent's widow into our grasp, and hold her captive until she is no longer capable of molesting us." The speaker's voice and face now became loud and heated.

"She may refuse to give us the opportunity, my dear," Dorrington languidly interposed.

"Then let her die," was rejoined in measured words, proceeding with energy —"the consideration is my only child, and of the two she must perish—aye, and I myself shall undertake the task, and accomplish it if he whose duty it is to guard the rights of his wife and son fails in the trust."

"What do you mean?" exclaimed her husband, turning in his chair.

"Ha, my lord! has conscience wounded you with the probe of truthfulness at my words; you know," she added, "that your hold of the Darecourt belongings shall be withered and decimated at the first fair contrast between foul fraud and bright omniscient truth."

"Upon my word, Fanny, you amaze me."

"Bah!" retorted his dissatisfied wife, "leave dissembling to others. Surely our child's weal is not to be frustrated by the continuance of any frail illusion. Go, my lord," she warningly continued, "while yet there is time, and render this righteous suitor powerless to wreak her well-merited vengeance upon us all."

"Dismiss the idea of merit, to which I lay but feeble claim," observed Lord Darecourt with a faint smile, "but tell me what you apprehend. I can see no occasion to notice the puny endeavours of a mere woman."

"A mere woman," echoed his spouse,

"has ere now stepped in and lit the torch of success, where self-redoubted champions of so-called men have tried and perished; besides," with increased energy, "she has Sir Mervyn Mervyn to pioneer her efforts."

"I am a lord, while he is but a baronet," was answered sarcastically.

"His powerful interest has already se-cured to her the help of the executive in prosecution of this claim, and in the removal of the unfounded charge against her banished husband."

"I do not owe my position either to him or the Government, Fanny."

"The publicity of the lawsuit will bring back your cousin even from the antipodes, provided he is still alive," she resolutely urged.

"The idea is sweetly Utopian, my dear," answered Lord Darecourt in a bantering vein; "but you overlook the impossibility of ousting a man in possession, and that man a rich lord."

"Yet, Dorrington, the most advanced and eminent of lawyers are already ranged on the side of our determined opponent."

"Yes," he responded in a drawling, listless tone; "like intoxicated fools they have become giddy with success, and will overbalance themselves in rushing against a wealthy nobleman."

Maddened at the levity he exhibited and the little effect her reasoning had, she shouted with a vehemence of voice and manner which irresistibly caused the two listeners to jump to their feet, confronting her.

"Drunkenness is the epilepsy of hell; but he who is of mankind born, and can look on content while his wife and child are being despoiled—the latter of even its birth-right—is beyond the reproach of the foulest fiend to be found within that charred, exhaustless catacomb."

The agent looked on meekly silent, but the muscles of his mouth revealed deep agitation, while the master of Darecourt stood regarding his spouse with a gaze of speechless wonder if not absolute alarm.

"Bring me writing materials," she authoritatively demanded after a short pause, drawing her chair to the table, not deigning to notice her husband's asto-nished expression. "Flynn, I can depend on you, if on no one else." She spoke with marked bitterness.

"That ye can, for me life, yer leddy-ship."

"I think so," with a slight hesitancy, proceeding in a commanding strain.

"You know where this Mrs. Lucy Dare-court lives ? "

" Yis, yer leddyship."

"Is it not at Howth ? "

" Yer leddyship's always right, bedad !"

" Then I will entrust you with this missive to deliver into her own hands."

" She wudn't accipt it from me, yer leddyship."

" Why not, pray, if you go as Lord Darecourt's representative ? "

" Ye'll pardon me, yer leddyship, bud I don't think as how she'd recayve it av his lordship himsel' wint."

" At any other time I would scorn to notice her—now I shall play the hypocrite until she is so effectually crushed, that even the spirit or desire to live is dead and entombed in her. Go, Flynn," she continued, rising as the middleman cautiously advanced, " have the long-boat manned,

and send the letter by one whom you can
trust, prepared to bring this self-asserting
widow back to-night."

"Back to-night," echoed her liege,
as the agent bowed and withdrew.

"I said so, my lord."

"What do you mean, Fanny?"

"To entice her to the wood of Feltram,
where no eye can see or ear listen to what
her future fate may be, which she herself
shall determine by the acceptance or rejection of my conditions."

Stepping back a pace or two, he observed,
in accents of sarcastic inquiry,—

"Ha! ha! Are you afraid of some one
at last, though that one be Lucy Darecourt?"

"Peace, driveling idiot!" was exclaimed
sternly. "I am only afraid of the day-
light revealing your fraud."

Dorrington sank upon the couch dejectedly, while laughing almost in his ear she continued with vicious disdain,—

"I look down in scorn upon you."

CHAPTER VI.

VERILY a profound change has come over
the *personnel* of the Dangan estates since
the period when we last presented them to
our readers' notice!   Contentment, peace,
and prosperity being the three charac-
teristics now visible to the most super-
ficial observer as the numerous tenantry
walk by, well-clad and well-looking.   The
cheery salutation "God save ye," manifestly arising from a light heart.   What
is the cause of this evident alteration?
Is it the open-hearted English baronet
figuring so largely in every object of real
philanthropy or his wife, for that he had

long since been married, seemed a condition inseparable from one of his rank and
appearance, or abandoning either of these
probable alternatives it might be that the
many acres had passed into other and abler
hands who thoroughly appreciated their
occupiers from an Irish stand-point. No,
a distinct negative must be returned to
these several conjectures. Sir Mervyn
Mervyn was as good and benevolent as
before, providing for each honest necessity of the holders of Dangan, still his
property, but he had been absent from
Ireland for years travelling on the Continent
and in America; hence it was not his active
hand that had wrought the general im-
provement, nor, however surprising it may
appear, was he yet married, indeed those
who knew him best asserted that he had
no intention of entering life's *rôle* of cares
as a Benedick. But the subject of these

opinions had secretly resolved within his heart of hearts, "If I can induce her to listen to me, I will;" but no, no, we must not anticipate.

The proximate and immediate source whence springs all this happiness and contentment upon that wide demesne is to be traced to the English wife of the repentant, reinstated Robert Arkwright, and the hands that were once raised against the agent in Cain-like enmity would now tear down with the enthusiasm of affection the faintest glimmer of even suspected evil to him before the apprehended wrong could become a reality. He lived to obliterate the remembrance of the past by a career of honest, virtuous clemency, and although the compatriots of his class and a few other individuals regretted and contemned him for his so-called cowardliness, the world at large applauded the resolute man who recognizing injustice had the courage to avow and flee its enticing pursuit.

Lucy Darecourt and the O'Grady were amongst his foremost friends, but Brien Flynn intuitively feeling that parallel lines can never meet—henceforth separated himself from "the milk an' wather rhanagayde," as he described him, adding with bitterness, "I'm sorry I iver put mesel' in the varmin's clutches."

While the Dangan deputy had grown grey-haired and somewhat marked by time, his employer, Sir Mervyn Mervyn, became broader and more compact—although assuming an air of contemplative gravity unusual in one of his temperament. As we now find him, he was sitting in the agent's comfortable drawing-room, taking his ease after varied multitudinous wanderings. The window blinds were closely drawn shutting out the banks of night-clouds rolling upwards from the sea, while the ruddy baronet and his trusted host drew their respective seats nearer to the welcome fire, the traveller sympathetically relating many of the startling incidents associated with the unavailing search in quest of Vincent Darecourt, and Robert Arkwright, reciprocating the chord of harmonious feeling then uppermost, told in return all that he knew concerning each item of mutual interest or local import happening during the absence of his guest.

" I am very glad," continued the younger man, " that my efforts with the executive have availed so fully as to secure the restoration of her property to Mrs. Darecourt."

" And the removal of the prohibitive bar against her husband," responded his listener.

"Which is of little use now, except as a personal gratification."

"Then, Sir Mervyn, you believe him to be dead?"

"Unquestionably, and to this fact may be ascribed my success with the government on behalf of his relict."

"I am truly sorry for her," observed the agent with a pained expression.

His employer answered in a more hopeful tone, — "Regret is useless, and as already announced to you, I have secured the services of the former solicitors to the Darecourt family to vindicate her claims as widow of the legitimate heir of the last lord."

"A righteous move," ejaculated Arkwright, his face losing its colour, "for never was fraud more patent than that whereby the present possessor usurped both title and estates," adding inquiringly,

"Do you think Mrs. Darecourt will prosecute her cause to the utmost?"

"Decidedly! The preliminary steps
have been taken, and she cannot now consistently retire from establishing the fact
of her husband's unsullied paternity if for
no other purpose."

"So soon," exclaimed the agent, the
hue on his face being of a very uncertain
shade now.

"Why not? right is right, and she
shall have what justly devolves upon her
as relict of the defamed, outraged Vincent," emphatically remarked Sir Mervyn
Mervyn.

"Is Mrs. Darecourt aware of all that I
represented to you?" was asked in a
modulated voice, as though the speaker felt
timid of himself.

"Not all, she will call here this evening
on returning from the city; do not be

afraid, Arkwright, banish this lingering
hesitation and unfold yourself fully, per-
forming a good, retributive action that
cannot fail to exalt you in her eyes as it
does in mine."

"True, Sir Mervyn, but only to think
that through Dorrington Darecourt, his
agent, and myself, she has hitherto lost so
much; even her husband perished a victim
to our damnable conspiracy." The peni-
tent speaker looked abashed upon the
floor.

"Rely on it, the rascals would have
found other means of accomplishing their
ends without your assistance, and it is a
judgment upon them that you were concerned in the plot, when now rising up
to vindicate justice at their deserved sacrifice."

"Yes, that is the one only consolation
to fall back upon, but it is a painful ordeal

having to confess to an injured woman who has suffered so long."

"You can judge yourself where to draw the line," counselled the baronet; "for which reason I did not proceed so far in the recital of what you confided to me as otherwise I should; but I forgot, where is the stranger I brought with me?"

"Among the servants, well taken care of, I assure you," the agent answered, with a meaning glance.

"He will prove one of our trump cards," responded Sir Mervyn Mervyn, with deep significance. "Indeed," he went on, "this evidence alone will be sufficient to establish our friend's position. Ha, here they come," as a knock resounded throughout the house, and almost immediately before either of the gentlemen could gain the doorway, Lucy Darecourt appeared, escorted by the senior partner in the firm of solicitors now acting for her. She was dressed in deep mourning, and seemed somewhat heated on entering the warm room, but this rapidly gave way to a settled, composed look of ineffaceable sorrow, while her expressive eyes pierced you through and through. And the Dangan agent felt it so when with face flushed by the light of anxious inquiry she quietly but measuredly observed as though it were demanding and entreating at the same time,—

"Mr. Arkwright, will you please to narrate all that you wish me to know respecting the Darecourt conspiracy so far as relates to my banished husband? Sir Mervyn Mervyn prepared this gentleman," indicating her lawyer, "and myself to expect as much."

Bowing in return to her melancholy smile, the baronet interposed, "Mr. Arkwright is already aware how deeply we sympathize with him, and applaud his determination to further the cause of justice, great though the trial may be personally, and the extent of the disclosure must be wholly governed by his private feeling in the matter."

The agent, however, needed little forbearance from his auditors; once the first sense of shameful reservation had vanished he succinctly placed the whole of Dorrington Darecourt and Brien Flynn's successful plot before them, as he knew of it, from its earliest to its latest phases.

Lucy listened to the clear recital with the utmost tranquillity, but its effect was different on the phlegmatic solicitor, who at the termination thereof exclaimed,—

" This, then, was what the nefarious Flynn darkly hinted at in my office; and when contemptuously declining further conversation I wrote to his employer, the late Lord Darecourt, nothing whatever came in reply, until we ceased to be connected with the family."

After an interval, during which Arkwright regained composure, the lady, addressing the scion of law, asked,—

"What do you think of the case now?"

"A fraud is a fraud, madam," was the logical reply.

"Do you contemplate any new step?" requested the baronet, seeing that the attorney was about to continue.

"The precept from the Court has already been issued and served upon the defendants, but my present purpose is to consider whether we cannot couple all the delinquents together on a charge of forgery, and although this unreal lord is in possession, we will easily reach him and the agent. The great difficulty being

to prove that this woman, Fanny Chalmers, was a party to the falsification
before or after her marriage. With the
evidence of this gentleman," pointing to
Arkwright, "and that of the man who
wrote the false papers, already forthcoming, there would be little to apprehend,
the only questions troubling me are at
what period of the scheme were these vile
conspirators married, and what has become
of the original deeds, which of course
they, in collusion with Flynn, abstracted,
substituting spurious ones in their
stead."

"You think there can be no doubt,"
he added, addressing the baronet, "of
the demise of this lady's husband?"

"Alas! none; all that is humanly possible I have tried for his discovery, or
that of his companion, Mr. Dillon, but
failed, and it was only when convinced of

the inutility of pursuing the search longer that I returned from America."

Lucy rewarded the speaker with a fervid look of gratitude.

" It would embarrass us considerably in prosecuting the case, were you, Sir Mervyn, unable to satisfy the Judge as to the impossibility of finding and producing Mr. Vincent Darecourt, and of the probability of his death."

" Do not say so," pleaded the young widow, with a voice pitiable in its soft, wailing, uncertain sound.

" Of course, dear madam," responded the fluffy man of law, thrown off his guard, " we require to be very practical in dealing with details which if unexplained to the satisfaction of the Court might seriously operate against us." The speaker now suggested it was time to depart, having nothing more to ascertain, except a clue

could be found as regards the date of
Fanny Chalmers' marriage, and the present *locale* of the genuine deeds."

" I shall put my trusted assistant, old
Dominick Sullivan, on the alert, who is
very likely to ferret out something to
our advantage," was volunteered by the
Dangan agent.

" If he displays as much discernment
and industry in this cause, as he did when
walking to Paris in his own, success is
certain," observed the baronet, nodding
and laughing good-humouredly towards
Arkwright.

They all now turn to the hall, at the
door of which stands Sir Mervyn Mervyn's
carriage, waiting to convey Mrs. Darecourt to her temporary home at Howth,
the intention being not to reoccupy
Nevillstown until the result of the im-
pending trial became known.

Warmly shaking hands with the solicitor and Arkwright, the baronet assisted Lucy to her seat in the elegant vehicle, and had placed his foot on the step following, when the report of fire-arms in close proximity was succeeded by a scream, and the oil lamp over the entrance fell smashed to atoms.

That cry came from a concealed figure crouching behind the hedge on the opposite side of the road, who had raised and presented the pistol at the widow lady entering the carriage; simultaneously with the explosion that would-be assassin shrieked with pain, the hand holding the weapon being broken at the wrist by a well-directed blow diverting the fell bullet from its destined victim. A low voice appreciably restrained reached the miscreant's ear, hissing, " Away, thou inhuman fiend, ere my itching fingers rob justice of its suspended wrath and sate themselves deep in thy unwomanly bosom."

"Quick," exclaimed the Outlaw, standing beside the equipage, "take her home, Sir Mervyn, there is danger in the wind."

"Who was that shot intended for?" Lucy Darecourt inquired, recovering from her alarm as she recognized the voice of O'Grady.

"An oil lamp, evidently," was hastily replied, raising his hat and smiling bitterly.

"Oh, come with us!" she urged.

But in accents of resolution, he answered, "Not now; necessity points me elsewhere."

The next moment the spirited horses dashed forward, while the Outcast of Wentworth Waste returned whence he had come, and vaulting over the hedge, stooped beside the fallen form of that person whose wrist

he had in his passion shattered, saying
easily, "I am at least a man, and rancour
with me is short-lived: give me thine
hand; would I had the power to spare thee
pain, but, alas! I can only assuage it;
necessity has long taught me the moral of
copying nature, and thus I will aid you."
Whereupon he gently laid the dislocated
member on a pillow of dry leaves, which
with adroitly improvised splints greatly
mollified the sufferer's pain. Then unresistingly he led her into the high road,
continuing, "I seek not to intrude myself,
go your way; but if you apprehend danger,
I will brave it for the sake of what you
ought to be—pure and stainless, that
which we expect in woman's nature."

Throughout the foregoing, the figure
confronting the speaker remained im-
passive, hence it was impossible for him to
note the effect his burning words created,

but he had not departed many paces from
her ere the exclamation half suppressed,
half spoken, reached him,—

"Oh, who can, he be? Alas! am I
recognized?"

Instantly that mighty form stood by her
side again, sternly declaring : " O'Grady,
the Outlaw, knows the false Lady
Darecourt."

CHAPTER VII.

" THE time and place are odd, but strange, dark deeds necessitate the avoidance of day-light; and although this one of mankind's most degraded types has been brought to the confession of guilt, neither the motive nor act can expunge the cruel deceit and hideous wrong so patiently endured.

" He promises to restore my darling Vincent's intercepted letters, and that he will no longer bar the way to my happi-ness. Oh! can it be true that my husband still lives, and that these usurpers will vacate their unhallowed possessions? Would I could be happy, ay, even in proportion as I have grown wretched!

"Existence is to me the synonym of perpetual sorrow, and will it not be fitly expiated in the service of my love?

"Baffled strategists brought to bay have often resorted to unheard-of extremes, and what may not this thrice perjured lord attempt?

"Let Dorrington Darecourt and his crafty partner but lay down their illicit, fraudulent gain, and I shall seek no advantage from the fallen foe, nay rather will I assist them to flee the country whose laws and society they have outraged, finding an asylum where they are unknown."

Thus mused the lorn Lucy, as, in that wild, pitiless storm she walked on alone and unattended, yet consciously sustained, to this interview with the supposititious owner of Darecourt.

Darkness reigned supreme on that

solitary, avoided road leading from Malahide to the wood of Feltram; and
although the wind startled every move-
able thing into a fictitious semblance
of existence, she proceeded, assured in
the conviction of personal safety, wholly
absorbed in pondering upon her long-
lost husband.

"I hope you have not been waiting,"
observed Lord Darecourt in an unsteady
voice, as he took his station under the
huge old elm-tree facing the hill whereupon stood the well-known windmill.

"I neither came to wait nor be detained," was answered in a firm, self-
asserting tone, contrasting strangely with
that of the previous speaker.

" The result shall compensate for the
unwonted journey."

" If I thought otherwise I would not be
here."

"Are you alone?" demanded the first arrival.

"Was it not a part of the compact that I should come by myself, even to the exclusion of my servant?"

"Yes, but I did not know if you had observed its literal fulfilment."

"My motto is never to deceive," was rejoined bitterly, with unmistakable emphasis, while her interviewer advanced still nearer, and folding his arms, said,—

"It would be obviously impossible, Mrs. Vincent Darecourt, to meet you for the first time—strange though the hour and place may be—and forego the opportunity of seeking to justify my actions in the past."

"Abandon this absurdity," she answered with severity; "all that can be urged will not alter what has been done, or its entailment of utter misery to me and

mine:" the lady became affirmative in
manner and tone, "come to the immediate issue, sir; what do you propose in
accordance with the statements whereby
you brought me here?"

"I will verify my representations," he
replied, "in their entirety; first of all"
(searching his coat) "you are doubtless
well acquainted with my Cousin Vincent's
handwriting."

"Yes," (wearily uttered) "I have seen
it too often, yet not often enough."

"Judge then, madam, are these his
letters addressed to you?"—unveiling a
parcel which he held towards the amber-
coloured, quivering lamp in his hand.

"Oh! thank Heaven, they are!" she
ejaculated; "and for these at least I am
your debtor,"—pressing the missives with
avidity to her lips.

"You must be satisfied, apart from

all suspicion, that I am a man of honour."

"Sir, let us proceed to the close: do not invite a contrast whereby your present actions must become tarnished by the memory of many past ones."

"I am content," he resumed; "and now entreat your serious attention to the proposition I resolved on making. Mrs. Vincent Darecourt, at best it is egregious folly to attempt to control destiny. Whichever of two courses you elect to pursue will decide whether the future is to become one of assured bliss or endless misery."

"I came prepared to solve my destiny," she responded unfalteringly, although the while appreciably drifting into a modified sense of alarm at the growing seriousness of her opponent's words and mien. Putting forth his face till it almost touched hers, he exclaimed quickly, in a voice that seemed to grow familiar to her astonished ears,—

"Sign this undertaking invalidating the lawsuit and acknowledging me to be the rightful Lord of Darecourt; in return I will assure to you the safety of Vincent, together with ample means wherewith to live luxuriously abroad; but refuse to do so and—"

"And what?" his surprised auditor demanded firmly.

"You will never behold him again— never—never, so help me—"

"Peace, blasphemer, nor dare defile my ears by such dishonouring words," she vehemently proceeded, gathering up her cloak to depart; "I tell you, man of fraud, that Heaven will right me despite your sordid machinations, and were it not that I received these cherished tokens of my

beloved husband from your hands I would
invoke the Almighty power on high to
abridge even the little time left wherein
you can despoil thy cousin and his
wife."

"Curse this pliant tongue," he shouted
angrily, "nor pity nor fear is in me but
you shall sign this acknowledgment.
Look, what are these prized mementoes
worth ? ha! ha! read them,"—and while
his discordant laugh rode out upon the
wind moaning through the swaying trees,
Lucy unfolded the paper marked as being
the last Vincent had written, and clasping
her hands upon her forehead almost immediately cried in heart-broken accents,—

"In mercy! spare me, spare me!"

There in her hand it lay, but too real
even to those true eyes, her husband's letter
traced upon his death-bed in characters
wherein effort and pain were clearly recog-

nizable. Leaving this world he bequeathed to his wife the bitterest reproaches for falsity, irrefragably established in her own intercepted handwriting then sullying the dying writer's troubled eyes. Appended was Eustace Dillon's well-remembered signature attesting the *bona fides* of the communication and the decease of Vincent Darecourt.

"Now, madam, what avails your puny efforts? and am I not foregoing my self-esteem in condescending to explain that which brought you to my feet, even while asserting a claim to be mistress of Darecourt?"

"Forego this," she urged; "I am crushed, broken-hearted."

But her informant was selfishly resolved on taking advantage of her helpless misery, saying,—

"There will be another time for your

grief, which is but natural; now let us become friends. Endorse this—"

Ere the sentence was finished she interposed inquiringly,—

"How could you just now offer upon certain terms to restore my husband to me if he were really dead?"

"I did, but—but," after a pause, "it was to show the more effectually how that for joy or sorrow you lay completely at my mercy."

"Thus playing the despot with my feelings," was coldly observed; "and surely if I am so worthless it is not becoming in you to stoop asking my signature to that document. No," she continued in a firmer tone, "he who is false in aught is ever untrue; take back your fraudulent creations, or leave them for the derision of night-fiends; the writing is truly that of my erring, misguided

Vincent, but I will still trust to the justice of innocence for retribution, while you, shameless, unmanly creature, vainly try to smother the gnawings of a perjured, forsworn soul." Whereupon she turned to retire while the enraged listener sprang forward in her path, shouting,—

"Stay! sign this paper, or you will never go hence alive."

"By the mercy of Heaven I shall not," that pale-faced woman answered fearlessly, continuing, "I will die sooner than sacrifice my husband's heritage and acknowledge your monstrous perfidy."

The speaker attempted to move while he kept before her crying out,—

"Flynn, Flynn, come forth at once."

"Ha! has the so-called Lord Darecourt need for the services of another as questionable as himself?" she remarked, in a stinging, taunting voice.

" Bring me the rope," was the mandate of the employer as his agent advanced.

" 'Tis here, me lord," the latter meekly replied.

" Then cast it around, and we will bear her to the mill yonder."

" Yis, me lord," the deputy responded, throwing one end of the coil, which his confederate caught.

" Do you seriously mean to harm me?" the lone widow asked, for the first time betraying real concern.

" Subscribe your name," retorted her antagonist, presenting the document, " or you shall not see daylight again."

" I dare you to the worst," she haughtily rejoined, folding her cloak and looking on calmly.

" Draw !" shouted the incensed Dorrington to his assistant, when Lucy immediately passed the encircling noose over her head. Infuriated at seeing her free, the supposed Lord Darecourt turned and raised his hand to grasp her, but suddenly he lay unconscious on the earth, while his coadjutor reeled back several yards and also fell.

"Oh, why is your untimely lot cast in with these evil-born cowards?" exclaimed the Outlaw despondingly, as, taking Lucy's arm in his, they both left Feltram's mystic wood.

CHAPTER VIII.

LUCY DARECOURT looked out from her
favourite alcove upon the shiny waves,
laving those rocky boulders which, as it
were, formed a trellis work around her
vigil height, where in loved solitude she
was wont to renew the sunny days of yore,
the thought uppermost in her pensive mind
at this moment being, what could the false
usurper of Darecourt mean by resorting
even to violence in an abortive attempt
to force her into a recognition of this
usurpation; but above all, how or by
what means did he obtain possession
of her husband's writing, which, alas! was

no simulation, but too, too real in its dire import?

"The lawyers have comforted me, it is true, by saying that the very audacity of the enterprise reveals its inherent weakness. Yet their lucid minds could not unravel the mystery attending the letter, except that, as they opined, it augurs the existence of a deeper plot than was comprehended, extending to some false detestable misrepresentation, which reached Vincent in his remote home wherever it may have been, causing him to reproach me even on his—but no, no," she suddenly exclaimed, " it is an impossibility. He would never be permitted to die without knowing how loyally my young life has grown old in the service of his memory. What other object have I ever held first in my bereaved heart but that one born of love—a pellucid, exclusive love that can only find its meed of necessary requital by knowing he survives in happiness." Then her musings embraced the devotion of the Outlaw. "How noble he is, how dead to all else but the conviction that he holds the right to guard me in fulfilment of his last words to my husband, and well is this trust redeemed, ay, even when unknown to myself. I should have fallen by the device of that equivocal impostor, Dorrington Darecourt, but for his timely aid; unthought of and unexpected, and panther-like he must have followed the trail while, forgetful of him, I wended my way to Feltram Wood. Was I not grateful to Sir Mervyn Mervyn when announcing his success with the Government, not merely in recovering my long forfeited property, but beyond this in securing such consideration for O'Grady, that did the latter bend his proud neck asking for pardon, the Crown would willingly grant it and rehabilitate him. Yet he steadfastly, even peremptorily, declines listening to a suggestion of humbling himself, however slightly, preferring instead to pursue that nomadic, wretched life.

" My darling Vincent," she continued to soliloquize, " wert thou here, would not thy earliest, deepest care be to preserve and honour him who has saved me from death, and whose fostering hand is this moment raised unseen to disperse all that would rob your Lucy of quietude ? "

A knock at the door caused the thinker to look round—her aunt (the companion of her retirement) had been dead some years, —when the faithful, if withal querulous, odd Margaret made her appearance, saying,—

" 'Tis thim boys wantin' the rush-light for the year kindled."

" Oh, certainly, Margaret, I really quite

forgot that this is the anniversary of the time-honoured holiday, send them to me," and rising, Lucy Darecourt went towards the porch, waiting the arrival of the villagers, who approached, preceded by the oldest man of their number.

This patriarch left the others waiting on the threshold while he walked to where Lucy stood, and kissing the hem of her dress, shouted through his toothless gums, "Three cheers for the lone lady av the hill," whereupon a chorus of vigorous approbation was sent up, which, although representative of the many, had at least one exception, testy old Margaret being heard objurgating,—

"Ye'd moither the divil wid yer onnathural schrayms."

"I am much obliged for your hearty salutation," responded the hostess with smiles, followed by the usual,—

" Hivin bless yer leddyship, yer own'll com back yit, 'tis far aff what God sinds."

" I'd like to sind ye far enof, anyhow," muttered the domestic, while her mistress observed, addressing the village Nestor,—

" Bring me the brand."

" 'Tis here, yer leddyship," he answered, presenting the rush-light.

She was known amongst the people as the " lone lady av the hill," and vain proved every effort to prevent their indulging in " her hanest dhue," always styling her, " Yer leddyship."

Lucy now applied a match to the igneous material, and handed back this flickering torch to the old man, saying,—

" May no darkness shroud this light
Upon our rocky shore ;
Nor wrong e'er conquer right
While full one year runs o'er.

The year will run, its morrow come,
   Moments ages push ;
In joy, not pain, return again
   With autumn's spectre rush."

"Hurra, hurra!" was universally exclaimed, and each receiving a silver coin
from the "lone lady," these visitors hoist
their pigmy emblems on high, departing in
single file down the zigzag shingly pass,
singing the foregoing traditional lines to
some melancholy chant, looking very
picturesque in the distance.

Lucy watched them with keen interest,
unmindful that Sir Mervyn Mervyn was
already in the room, he being a privileged
visitor at all times, and, indeed, it may be
recorded of aged Margaret that he never
came too often, for as she expressed it,—

"He's a habit av dhrivin' his hand into
his breeches pockit, thryin' to git me to
say, 'No,' bud plaze God, I'll take the con-

sayt out av his purse many a time afore 'twill cum to that ingratithude."

" I am sorry to disturb your reverie, Mrs. Darecourt, but may I ask the mean-ing of this rustic pageant ? " inquired the baronet at her side.

" Oh," she answered, while holding out her hand, " I did not know you were here ; " it is an ancient custom in these parts that on a certain day a rush shall be lit by the occupier of the highest house on this hill and handed to the oldest man in the village, who afterwards, in company with his fellows, parade its streets, making merry over the close of the autumn season."

" The autumn season ! " he echoed, " I fail to see the relevancy."

" It is easily accounted for, winter is not supposed to begin until this light has been kindled, as you probably witnessed."

"A strange custom, indeed," remarked the baronet.

"It is harmless simplicity, and on this account I rather incline to foster it," Lucy observed with a pleased look.

"Capital philosophy, Mrs. Darecourt," was replied approvingly.

"There is very little of unselfishness in our wonted pleasures, Sir Mervyn, and I fear now-a-days the motive too often dictates the act; but, oh, what sound is that?" she exclaimed, hurrying towards the window, and drawing back the heavy curtains while she looked out, her auditor following.

Margaret hereupon came into the room with lights, which, however, her mistress silently motioned to be taken back, as bending forward, Lucy Darecourt seemed to drink in every iota of the sweetly-phrased song ascending upwards from

the granite-bound foundation beneath her
feet—

"Thou'lt rend my heart no more:
   I bid thee go, I bid thee go;
Life's darkest hour is o'er:
   Thou'rt false, I know : thou'rt false, I know.
Thy face e'en wears its wonted smile:
   It shall not be, it shall not be;
Nor seeming grief, nor luring wile,
   Can alter me, can alter me.

"Thou'st fool'd me to the last:
   My faith was warm, my faith was warm;
To stem the world's rude blast,
   I've braved its scorn, I've braved its scorn.
But like the dead sea fruit
   That mocks the sun, that mocks the sun,
Thou'rt lifeless in thy truth,
   And we are done, and we are done.

"As Time drifts on its seething course,
   Enfeebling thee, enfeebling thee,
I wish thy breast a thought no worse
   Than think of me, than think of me.
Perchance the halcyon days of yore,
   Their semblance green, their semblance green,
Will waft the myrtle from the shore,
   Where peace is seen, where peace is seen."

The theme and melody seemed to float over the lady in some mystic fashion, and being ended she impulsively closed the window, retiring to a seat seldom used in the distant corner, when the servant re-entered, bearing wax tapers.

"Why are you thus signally despondent?" inquired Sir Mervyn Mervyn in a soft, emotional, low voice, perceving his hostess with her face hid in her hands, oscillating from side to side.

"Oh," she wailed without looking up, "I am so wretched, so heart-broken, something in that refrain causing me to think it was Vincent's unfounded reproach, sung in his rebuking accents of sadness."

"A phantasm pure and simple, be assured," was responded as the speaker drew his chair near, the silence for a while being undisturbed, save for those monitory unfailing strokes of time's tell-tale, the clock.

Hardly able to repress the swelling tumult within him, her companion at length asked in a would-be-grave manner,—

"Mrs. Darecourt, when will this continued sorrow cease, that your friends may see you even as you should appear, joyously content, thereby making others happy?"

"Ah," she answered dejectedly, preserving that drooped, quiescent attitude, "never again; my sun of life is set, and all the specious gilding on this world's toys of pleasure cannot wean me from the remembrance of the past; it is thus and only thus I care to live."

"This is sheer madness, surely there is some one on earth who by an imperishable devotion will soften and lessen your grief, or mayhap in the long future beget an affection rivalling, if not eclipsing, the former love?"

"Never more, never more," was slowly and mournfully returned.

"Oh, Lucy," he pleaded, bending before her, "give me the right to call you that name, obliterating this current of intemperate woe; let me live to realize your dream of earthly bliss," and unresistingly he held her hands, but the next moment she looked at him solemnly and warningly, while her voice partook of deep apprehension, saying,—

"You have been so chivalrous throughout the many years of my lonely suffering, that I dare not utter what I feel at this moment; still generously pity and forgive me when I declare we can never be other than friends, real, true, and sincere; for will not gratitude always lead me to you? Yet, oh look, look," she vehemently exclaimed, while starting up from the chair, as the baronet in trepidation rose from the carpet whereon he had been kneeling. "See, see, thank heaven, it is Vincent, my own darling husband," and she rushed to the window, whereat her suitor observed the very pale, serious face of a man, who suddenly disappeared when the lady approached.

"Come to me," she cried aloud, bursting wide open the casement, "come to me, Vincent, it is your wife who calls, do not leave her. Ah, can you forsake your own Lucy? I saved your life, why dost thou turn away? Have I not too long endured an unequal struggle for you alone? Come back to me, Vincent, come back!"

Sir Mervyn stood close to her, awed into silence by that reproachful eloquence of despair, and both now bend their ears listening in anxious expectation, still nought was heard save the wash of the dark waves breaking on the rocks below, or the night psalm of some distant plover and wild curlew.

"Hark!" said Lucy Darecourt breathlessly, pointing with her finger towards the place whence that agitating song had recently proceeded, and wherefrom at this moment the same deep musical voice in sustained, robust accents, vociferated,—

"False one, farewell for ever."

· The calm wind bore the awful sentence upwards, followed by a plash of the waters, and, as they thought, a second yielding of the waves; but no, nothing, nothing was discernible beneath that shroud of ebony black desolation.

"Oh, Father! take me hence, my heart is broken," faintly uttered the bereaved woman, reeling helplessly backwards.

CHAPTER IX.

"THERE remain but two clear days before the Darecourt trial," observed the Outlaw regretfully, sitting opposite Robert Arkwright. "Still the genuine deeds have not been obtained, and without them there may be extreme difficulty in establishing the claim."

It was remarked of late that O'Grady had become very abstracted, if not really irritable, as though some new unforeseen trouble had arisen, bearing him down with its unexplained burthen.

"I know you are too painstaking to have omitted anything, but might they not be in the same apartment, yet differently placed to others?" Sir Mervyn Mervyn's agent inquired.

"An impossibility," was tartly responded, "I closely searched every nook and corner therein, getting nothing for my pains but blue mould and cobwebs."

"What a courageous act to explore even the strong room in Darecourt Castle," said his host, but unmindful of the personal compliment O'Grady proceeded,—

"Something must be done this very night; to-morrow may be regarded as our last day for action, and I have undertaken to satisfy two strangers who are interested in the results that these documents will be forthcoming."

"But the difficulty is how to begin," suggested Arkwright.

"Yet it shall be overcome. I have

never been unfaithful to a promise, and my personal assurance is pledged to find these original Darecourt deeds on or before the second day from hence."

"I fail to see how you are to succeed, much as success is desired."

"Nor do I," echoed the visitor, when both relapsed into silence, musing upon and anticipating the result of the celebrated suit.

"Call the nephew of the Darecourt agent," said O'Grady suddenly, adding, "he seems a reliable fellow, and if we can get him to operate upon his degraded relative, whilst close at hand, fear will overawe Brien Flynn, or I am signally mistaken."

"I think your judgment is as usual very sound," the Dangan deputy uttered reflectively. "My own knowledge of this Roddy would lead me to trust him in a marked degree, for he had every incentive to go over to the opposite side."

" True, but I trust no one unreservedly," was replied with an emphatic gesture of caution, as the aforesaid nephew of the " grinder " entered.

" Be seated," enjoined Arkwright, pointing to a chair, whereupon the Outlaw addressed the late arrival, inquiring,—

" Your motive, I believe, in coming to assist the cause espoused by Sir Mervyn Mervyn is solely to do good."

" Yis, yer honour."

" Although it includes the exposure of your uncle, Brien Flynn ? "

" There's no gra bethune us, nor iver will be."

" Has he injúred you in any way ? "

" In throth he has, he tuck me from me well-payin' gayme av law work, an' whin gettin' all he wantid I wor shipped aff to Ameriky an left to stharve, till the masther gev me a helpin' hand. An', plaze God, I shall do whativer I hav promised Sir Mervyn, ay to the lasth pinsworth."

"This sounds well," exclaimed his interrogater, continuing, "are you prepared to meet Flynn at once?"

"To tell ye trooth, sir, av it warn't that I moight be shuspicted av underhand work in goin', me wish is to see him afore we meet an the thryal. Who knows bud I may draw the few pounds he sthill owes me niver havin' sint any to Ameriky."

"Then you shall see him, and on this very night; but I must accompany you, the errand being one of no slight danger."

"As ye like, sir, I'm contint. Anythin' to prove I'm not undesarvin' the kindness Sir Mervyn show'd me."

"Which I will gladly undertake to continue," supplemented the baronet's agent, "only proceed resolutely to the close of this trial, thereby making me as well as Sir Mervyn Mervyn anxious to become of permanent use to you."

"Thin, gintlemin, all I can say is, put anythin' afore me, an' trust me I've had enof av the world through belayvin' me purty relativ' Brien, much good may his dhirty money do him."

Some hours later, four men walked resolutely along the Artane road, carefully avoiding the isolated habitations on the lonely way, until they approached the "Darecourt Arms," where, as we have previously read, Eustace Dillon's brother was relating his perturbed dreams to the company and "Mine host," strangely corroborated by the latter, when a face at the reeking window, like unto the late heir of Darecourt, violently startled them from their composure, tobacco, and whisky.

The guests who had rushed out in pursuit of that spectral appearance returned to the village inn disappointed, not knowing that the subject of their hot chase hastily joined his three companions in advance, and that at a signal the quartette crossed the boundary of Darecourt, hiding in the well-wooded enclosure on its inner side.

"Remain here," suggested O'Grady, "until I return ; note who enters or leaves the avenue, but do not show yourselves. Roddy, follow me," addressing Flynn's nephew, and both were soon after out of sight, the Outlaw in advance.

Avoiding the Castle, they clambered through the thick copse, and skirted the hedges, until reaching the rear of the building, where the extensive pleasure-garden terminated.

"Wait a moment, and I will give you a helping hand," observed the leader, making a herculean spring, thereby gaining the top of the high wall, which his observer regarded with amazement, though he was immediately afterwards beside him, having been lifted lightly thereto by the immense muscular power of that man.

The attuned ears of the latter at once discovered the approaching sound of distant voices, and, dropping into the close ivy, he seized his follower, saying,—

"Silence! there are people coming this way."

"I hear nothing," replied Roddy in a whisper.

"But I do," was answered decisively, and both lay concealed in their umbrageous covering.

" This is a secluded place," observed a person beneath them.

" Id is, yer leddyship," followed from a second individual.

" Tell me now," proceeded the first; " we shall meet no more until the trial decides our fate, but speak plainly,—Where are the missing deeds to be found? Mind, no prevarication, and, as promised, I will give you the open draft for five thousand guineas that I took from you on the day of the late lord's demise, which I have scrupulously held unused since, for some such pressing emergency as is now presented to us."

" Yer leddyship shall hear all, bud ye'll recollict, not even the lord himsel', nor any other sowl is to know excipt yer leddyship."

" Not one."

" Yer leddyship won't ax to touch the

parchments till the joory hav' com' to a sittlemint?" The narrator inwardly thought, "I'll be there afore ye."

"Not until the jury have arrived at a settlement as you say, Flynn." Her "leddyship" privately resolving to secure them forthwith.

"Thin av yer leddyship 'll kindly sit down here," pointing to an arbour, " I'll tell ye everythin'."

"Very well," was answered, " go on, sir."

"As a young leddy, yer leddyship may remimber to hav' herd av a cilebrated fire near the bridge, this side av the river ?"

"I do not remember."

"Oh, yer leddyship will av ye think," urged the male speaker, continuing, " the white lookin' house wor burned down, where a half-witted craythure naym'd Molly MacCarthy losth her life."

" Yes, yes, I have a slight recollection of something of the sort, but what has this to do with these deeds ? "

" Yer. leddyship is a throifle too anxshus," was replied in a semi-admonishing voice; " kindly listhen, an' ye'll see where the papers are hid."

" That I intend to do without delay," she silently muttered.

" Whin the roof wor burned," he proceeded, " they thried to foind the remayn's av that odd fish, Moll, bud cudn't, an' gev up the sarche; now whin I wantid to sthow away the parchmints, the thought kem into me hed, there's no sphot haf so safe as a coffin."

" What do you mean ? " his auditor passionately demanded.

" Only this, yer leddyship, I put all the dockiemints in a led coffin, an' had thim berry'd in Richmond Churchyard, the lasth grave nixt the canal an the right hand side, where the shilter is for the clargyman; there they are safe an' sound, wid the nayme av Moll MacCarthy bloomin' over thim,—the viry lasth plaice in the world she'd think av goin' for thim," the agent composedly considered, while his noble mistress congratulated herself, musing,—

"They are so secure in the earth, that he cannot possibly imagine I will seek their recovery without his aid, although I shall certainly do so to-morrow night.'

" An original strange interment, indeed," observed Lady Darecourt aloud, " but, perhaps, it was the wisest course after all ; here is the draft for five thousand guineas, as arranged," adding, " of course there is no doubt but that all the documents are in the coffin ? "

" Ivery wan, yer leddyship, that wor

brought from the sthrong room are there, as ye'll foind whin I cum to take thim up in yer prisince."—"I niver shall," he thought gleefully.

"You will not," she was inwardly resolved, saying in a satisfied tone, "This information is satisfactory. I will now retrace my steps; good night, Flynn, and fear not the results, we must conquer; if all else fails, a bullet shall accomplish the object, although my last shot was not a success," the female looked wistfully towards her hand in splints.

"Good noight, yer leddyship; wid the papers in our possesshun we can't be bayte."

"My possession," she soliloquized, as his last words reached her, while closing the postern gates.

"Ha, ha, ha!" exclaimed the veracious agent when left to himself, "the deeds ye'll

niver see; no, to-morrow at dark I'll be
there to clare thim away, ay, an' I'll sill
thim to the highest biddher, ha, ha, ha;
five thousand guineas also; com 'let me
look an yer illigant self, me bewty," holding the monetary draft in both hands, the
enthusiast kissed it, passionately uttering,
"Oh, what need I care now, I'll laff whoiver cries, shure the piper's ped alriddy,
—up wid ye," he added, in increased jubi-
lation. "I've herd there wor manna sint
to the Israylites in the dissirt, bud how
many five thousands iver com down, even
in a lord's garden, ha, ha, ha. Up ye'll go,
ay, to the virry sky, an' say yer moin in
sphite av heavin," waving the paper over
his head.

"Blasphemous liar, it's mine," came
from the top of the wall, as the valuable
security was nimbly clutched from his loose
grasp.

"Who are you?" groaned the crafty middleman, not daring to look up.

"An angel sent to avenge your wickedness," he heard retorted, and Brien Flynn fell upon his knees, weeping bitterly.

CHAPTER X.

WE have already seen in earlier pages that
the mysterious stranger who occasioned
so much unconcealed surprise to the good
people of Swords had taken his way
through the city of Dublin, avoiding its
principal streets, and successfully passed
over the boundary of the Richmond
Cemetery by means of a skilfully cast rope
from the opposite side of the wall.

Alighting at the base thereof, he found
his three companions of the previous night
awaiting him.

" Ha, thrice welcome indeed ! " observed
O'Grady.   " Now we will commence."

"Layve the job to me, yer honour," said Roddy, throwing off his jacket and gripping one of the spades lying against a headstone.

"I shall bear my part therein," proffered the unknown gentleman from Swords, but the Outlaw waved him to his side, saying,—

"It is only child's play; besides, I want to speak of last night's exploit, and the Darecourt agent's five thousand guineas."

"Ha, ha!" was unitedly laughed in *sotto-voce* accents, each being alive to the necessity for secrecy in their present task.

"I wondher how me uncle feels afther his palaver wid the hanest angel," urged Roddy, while he and the fourth silent individual went briskly to work, pick and shovel, observing strict time in close, measured pace.

"Keep a sharp look-out," ordered the

Outlaw, as with the stranger from Swords he paced to and fro.

The latter resumed, "You do not suppose there was any dissimulation on Flynn's part?"

"None whatever,"

"And that the veritable instruments are in this coffin?"

"Undoubtedly."

"What a deep scoundrel he must be to devise such a hiding-place."

"I rather applaud the idea," responded O'Grady, "for is it not the last corner on earth where a search would be thought of?"

"The wretch who is capable of resorting to such extremes is qualified for any dastardly action, and thus I am apprehensive that he but cheats this false woman of Darecourt into believing the real deeds are here."

" He could not impose upon her were he even so minded, nor is there a question as to the papers being in this grave; indeed, so accurate was he in his lucid description that almost at once I made out the situation on arriving in advance of you."

" Which is both corroborative and comforting; with the evidence of Arkwright as opposed to Flynn, this relative of the Darecourt agent, who wrote the noxious deeds, and, above all, the production of the originals themselves, the case seems clear enough, and I shall be glad when it is ended, that once more I am free and unfettered to go where duplicity is unknown and a false love unheard of."

" Hold, hold ! " interrupted his auditor deprecatingly; " you are wrong in these mad conjectures."

" Yet you neither could or would justify their cause," the stranger inquired.

"There we agree; but trust me the whitest lily in nature's widest domain is not a whit purer than she whom you so unfairly suspect."

"I would cheerfully undergo my life's perils anew could I think thus," the former vehemently replied.

They now confront the two figures, half-hid in the grave, who, with unabated vigour and unmindful that the walls thereof were not secured, went deeper and deeper therein to the rise and fall of these delving implements impelled by willing hands.

"I hope you are not over-exerting yourself?" observed the unknown from Swords in a concerned voice to Roddy's assistant in the digging.

"No thank you, it will soon be finished," was returned, Flynn's nephew noticing that these were the only words he had heard from his confederate, before whom he felt somewhat embarrassed, as silently they swayed to the warming task.

The Outlaw and his *confrère* resumed their leisurely walk, keeping a sharp lookout for anything unforseen.

A few moments had flown away unnoticed and unheeded between them, when O'Grady suddenly said,—

"I have had such a strange, unaccountable presentiment of late, whereby my future life shall be governed, that I long for the successful termination of this enterprise."

"Do not forget that in all concerning your prospects I am interested heart and soul," the other heatedly responded.

"I am not insensible to your kind intentions, although undeserved, but I hardly know how to fathom the currents recently flowing from my line of reasoning."

"It is time to resolve on a career befitting you, for surely," spoken with sadness, "this wandering life must have run its course. Leave the country with me."

"Neither of us will leave the country," was decisively rejoined by the Outlaw. "Nay," he continued, repressing his companion's movements, "I know what you would urge, but it is futile; while as regards myself, I am fast settling into a determination of abandoning my hard, untoward life, and of seeking an asylum in solitude and obscurity."

"You would not go abroad to follow that mode of existence which you have for years resorted to at home?" inquired his listener.

"No," was quickly replied, "my foot shall never show its heel to poor old Ireland; loved clime of my happy youth and desolated manhood, thou wilt not deny the lorn Outcast the shelter of a grave in the land of his heart; but hush, what is that?" and dropping to the earth the agitated speaker listened, then, eagerly rising, softly motioned to his companion to follow, and speedily they returned to the grave wherein the assiduous labourers had already revealed a leaden coffin to which at each end ropes were now firmly affixed.

" Quick," whispered O'Grady in a sharp, clear manner, " up with you, there are footsteps coming this way."

And immediately afterwards all four lay concealed behind a low hedge, the leader keeping in front with his hat pressed forward on his temples, the coat buttoned close round his throat, and lips and hands rigidly fixed, which those watching him felt betokened a determination to succeed in the nocturnal undertaking at any sacrifice.

After a short suspense they noticed three figures approaching, pioneered by one who groped about looking for some as yet undiscovered object.

"'Tis strange anyhow, dark an' all as id is, I can't make id out," exclaimed the foremost of the last arrivals.

"Make out what, Misther Flynn?" was interrogated.

"The grave," he answered with asperity, instantly afterwards exclaiming, while regarding the new-dug earth and the leaden coffin below, "Oh, blood an' thundher, bud she's bin here afore me an' got the prishus dockiemints!"

"What does he mayne?" inquired the third individual.

"Dockiemints is the nayme av the berry'd person," the latter muttered seriously.

Here the conversation was peremptorily concluded, the three explorers being lifted with the utmost ease, and precipitated in miscellaneous confusion on the metal structure beneath.

" Where am I, who are ye ? " ascending from their leader in accents of terror.

" You are in your grave, and I am the angel of vengeance," a voice sternly replied from above.

" Oh, Lord, save me, save me ! " feebly screamed the former, almost bereft of speech through extreme fright. " Lift me out," he added in palsied tones, " an' I'll forsake me evil ways an' repint ! "

" Don't let him commit the sin av murther in layvin us behind," pleaded his junior partners in the pit.

" Be jabers, I think so much av ye, Mister Flynn, 'twill be no ayzey matther for the angel himsel' to git ye out av me hands," whereupon the speaker seized the prostrate agent under his vest.

"Hands aff!" shouted the assailed.

"Bedad, an' that sayme's jist what I won't do. The angel may hav the coat, bud the breeches is moine."

"Why so?" asked the remaining occupant of the unearthly tenement.

"Lord presarve us! shure av the angel keeps daycint company he can't take him home widout a covern, so I'll hould an to the onminshunables."

"Open that coffin!" demanded O'Grady in tones of authority, "and hand up the papers you have falsely stolen and concealed therein."

He thought probably that there was a spring in it known only to the deputy, and the conjecture proved to be correct, as, turning to obey the mandate from on high, Flynn ejaculated,—

" Oh, wurra, wurra, shure 'tis the day av judgmint ! "

" The grater nicessity for a daycint pair av breeches," responded the middleman's unyielding admirer.

" Let me go ! " exclaimed his victim, revealing an opening in the coffin 'neath the flashing rays of a dark lantern.

" Let him go," echoed the voice from above.

" His room id be pleasanther nor his company av he'd layve the onminshunables."

" Give me your hands," was interrupted, and instantly the agent stood alone in the grave, as " Cup-o'-Tay," and Tom, of clock renown, vacantly recognized the patriot, to whom they pleaded,—

" We didn't know what job he wantid us for."

Repressing the intended explanation, however, the Outlaw enjoined,—

"Haste, send up every paper in that unlawful coffin."

"Thin will I be forgivin'?" inquired Flynn, feebly gathering the documents together.

"I shall not visit you again," was vouchsafed in reply.

"Ah, thank ye for that sayme," proceeded the prisoner in relieved tones, "bud, angel, won't ye save me whin ye git the articles?"

"The lot of man is to die," flowed succinctly from above.

"Bud shurely not widout the devarshun av a wake, snuff, whisky, and coortin," interrupted Cup-o'-Tay in deploring accents.

"Up with the papers, or I will—"

"No don't, angel, av ye plaze; there they are," presenting the prized parchments, adding, "now, angel, hav marcy an' a poor sinner."

" 'Tis false, you are a rich one," came towards him from on high.

"Not now," was answered in despair, "these writin's ye've got layves me as hard up as a one-legged parson."

"You're not so poor as your natural relative, Roddy, whom you induced to go to America, and left to perish."

"Oh, angel, yé know all me sins, what shall I do, what shall I do?"

"Mortal, make suitable restitution."

"Ah, angel dear, 'twud take a good constitushun to sthand in a coffin as I hav don," pleaded the suddenly devout man, with a tremor.

"Lie down in it," interrupted Tom.

"He's ben lyin' all his life," added Cup-o'-Tay.

"Your draft for five thousand guineas is gone," reached the delinquent from that same unswerving source beyond.

"I wish, angel, a draught id com' into this hole; I'm out av breth."

"The linth won't shute ye nayther, 'tis a small-sized coffin," volunteered Tom.

"Your conduct is unearthly," exclaimed the supposed one of the other world.

"Alas, angel, me posishun isn't," was the deputy's melancholy response, continuing—"The lanthorn's nearly out."

Unheeding, however, the first voice resumed, "I have reckoned up your debt and sent the draft to Roddy."

"Ah, angel, I hav' a Roddy rick'ner, an' 'twill take som' time makin' out the balance he'll owe me."

"Consider the wrong you have done in taking your nephew in."

"Angel, an uncle's allowed be law to take ivery wan in."

"The law should have provided for releasing an uncle; but, hush, what sound is that?" Again the Outlaw bent to the ground, and quickly recovering his erect position, said softly,—

"Hide, there are persons at hand."

"Alas, I'm hid alriddy," thought the middleman, as he sat himself down upon the metallic counterfeit.

"This is the direction he gave," uttered a female voice, "yet I see no memorial corresponding with his description;" she walked on, followed by two men disguised, ready to commence the labour of exhumation.

Suddenly the foremost of these three stood transfixed, as right beneath in that open space she perceived Brien Flynn seated with his head bent forward upon his chest, while the light of a lamp revealed an open lead coffin wherein there was nothing.

"Wretch, dissembler," escaped from

the enraged woman's white lips, " where are
those deeds that you promised, for which I
paid you five thousand guineas ? "

"Ah, yer leddyship," he demurely answered, " even in me grave ye won't let
me rest."

" Where are the papers ? " she inquired
fiercely.

"An angel fancied thim," was composedly answered.

" Madman," the former continued, livid
with anger, "return my money."

" The same hanesth angel tuck that
too."

"Am I dreaming;"—the speaker was
now fairly beside herself with passion—
demanding, "who put you there ? what are
you going to do ? "

"Unfortunately the same obleegin' angel
put me here, an' excipt yer leddyship helps
me, I'll be dead afore me time."

"You will be in ——; but there," she said restraining herself, "I must get you out, if but to show how I can revenge myself on those who dare deceive me," motioning to her two male assistants who stood mutely looking on ; they kneel down, and stretching forward, grasped the agent by the head, neck, and shoulders, commencing to draw him upwards. Not being a young and active man this task required great exertion, however they had just succeeded in bringing him to the surface, when suddenly, from on every side around there rose up the most hideous yelling, followed by the braying of asses, howling of dogs, mewing of cats, grunting of pigs, snorting of animals, and every conceivable discordant sound, accompanied by showers of earth and sand, while the adjoining bushes and hedges shook frantically.

Irresistibly the unfortunate deputy was allowed to fall heavily backwards upon the unyielding coffin. Her ladyship and confederates cutting pitiful figures, fleeing as fast as their limbs would carry them, forgetful of all but the burning desire to escape from the terrible pandemonium, peal after peal of unrestrained laughter breaking from the Outlaw and his associates at their successful simulation of contentious nature.

At last, helping the Darecourt agent forward, they all escaped over the outer wall of the churchyard just as the sleepy watchman began to exclaim, " What the divil does the daymon hubbub mayne ? "

CHAPTER XI.

THE day broke on which the trial for the possession of the title and estates appertaining to the Lord of Darecourt was to take place.

Everyone and everything seemed gladdened by the joyous sun shining with unwonted power, as though presaging the victory of right over wrong in that much-debated, fierce feud between two branches of the ennobled family. Each point of advantage remained tabulated and labelled within the King's Bench securing the prized place for some favoured occupant, while · in the outer hall of that magnificent pile

on Ormond Quay known as the Four
Courts the wedged-in masses had been
gathering from early morn waiting the
moment when the Hall of Justice would
open, thereby reflecting the active, absorb-
ing interest manifested in the issue of
the "grate thryal."

Dublin looked cheerful and gay, as is
its custom on fine days, but there was an
unmistakable paucity in the number of
passengers and sight-seers enjoying the
usual promenade from St. Stephen's Green
across the City by old Trinity, past that
chef-d'œuvre in architecture the Houses of
Parliament, now the Bank of Ireland,
through Westmoreland Street, thence over
Carlisle Bridge to the further end of that
princely *boulevard* Sackville Street.

Not that even an inconsiderable fraction
of those now absent from the public
resort could or would have been admitted

into Court, but none the less they traversed the line of the Quays or Dame Street in the hope of hearing how the " case " progressed.

Barristers of renown sought out their privileged seat, taking precedence according to rank over less fortunate sons of the law; and more than one retired legal lord was seen housed upon the bench, to witness the *dénouement* of the notorious Darecourt action.

That the heroine of over a dozen years ago, who had recklessly imperilled her life for a stranger, was now the petitioner as wife or widow of this stranger whose end none could yet clearly define, yielded material enough to warrant an expectant crowded audience; but when it became widely known that the popular English baronet, Sir Mervyn Mervyn stood in some way associated with the claimant, and even further, that the brave celebrated outlaw O'Grady actively assisted on her side, the feeling of interest developed into one of absolute anxiety to ascertain which party gained the day.

General sympathy went with the petitioner, as at once became evident when she emerged from the handsome, well-known equipage of the baronet who conducted her into Court, the current observations of the applauding observers being somewhat as follows :—

" Arrah ! mam, what'ill ye take an' save me loife ? "—good humouredly inquired.

" Me malidictshun an her av she'd be sich a fool as to thry," spontaneously rejoined.

" How far 'ill yer malidictshuns carry ?" the first speaker repeated.

" The linth av me fist—will that shute ye ? "

" Av ye com' widin sthrikin' distance I'll giv' ye the complimints av the sayzon for an answer ;—bud, murther, isn't she a bewtay oud-an'-oud ! "

" Oh ! a wondher intirely," assented the good-tempered belligerents, while Lucy Darecourt, pale but composed, took up her station facing the bench.

" There's the mayley badger ; look at his pimpled hed."

" A lord, how are ye?—Tuppince hay-pinny for the toitle."

" Make room, here's the moryah av a leddy, she's grateful to ' Ould Nick ' for the husband he sint her, hurroosh, hurroosh, hiss, hiss, hiss."

" They can't even appear daysint an other people's money," saluted the possessor of Darecourt and his wife while forcing their way inwards.

Lucy and Fanny were separated by a

short partition only; but though the former maintains a freezing yet becoming hauteur, the latter casts furtive glances towards that once bosom friend, hating her more bitterly for the admiration her pensive face and *distingué* air commanded.

The Lord-Lieutenant is represented by his Excellency's reappointed aide-de-camp, Colonel Bagshot, who seems to be a very gentlemanly old man indeed; still, despite his repeated efforts at conversing, Lucy declines to surrender her studied reserve, not having forgotten the " fly-boat " incident, while thereupon others exhibit a most convenient memory.

The well-known confidential agent of Darecourt, Brien Flynn, Esq., has not yet appeared, having become suddenly indisposed, but he will attend later on during the day.

It were idle to reproduce the stereotyped

speech of the claimant's counsel, which failed in the expectations of many, as instead of venturing on a *résumé* of the unusual, indeed sensational, incidents connected with the suit, he abruptly abridged it, exclaiming by way of peroration—

"My lord and gentlemen, never was a case simpler yet more irrefutable in fact than ours, and this vile fraud, detestable as deception is at all times, becomes heinous before God and man when you remember that through it one of Ireland's noblest, most intrepid of women has lost a devoted husband whom she rescued from the deep,"—suppressed cheering—"that thereby she was for a long period despoiled of every means of sustenance; yea, that to this unnatural crime, and to it alone, she owes her career of over twelve long weary years of sustained suffering and silent, unknown woe, the authors whereof

defile the temple of unsullied justice in
the persons of this spurious lord and his
unmarried wife."

Great commotion followed the latter
statement, even the Judge involuntarily
forgetting his usual decorum gazing with
curiosity upon Fanny, who, be it honestly
noted, bore the scrutiny well, while Dorrington looking furiously at the heated
advocate, vociferated,—

"It is a false, monstrous lie; we are
married, here is the certificate"—handing
up the official document to the bench.

·This spontaneous and manifestly genuine
act turned the scale in favour of the
possessors of Darecourt; indeed, the lady
revived amazingly, until having ended a
short consultation with his instructing
solicitor, the petitioner's counsel rose
again, and addressing the court, said,—

"My lord, I call upon you to impound

that document,"—indicating the tendered certificate, adding, "I will now produce my witnesses," whereupon every trace of resistance on the female defendant's part seemed to become evanescent and void.

With the assent of the Court the question of handwriting was first disposed of. Expert followed expert, each unhesitatingly maintaining that the writing which the present male accused admitted to be his was identical with that in the letters found at the residence of Eustace Dillon, who, together with Vincent Darecourt was thereupon arrested, afterwards regaining their liberty, as we have previously read, through the assistance of O'Grady.

"I will not seek," observed the eminent lawyer, "to justify this act of rescue and flight which led up to the catastrophe of Lord Darecourt's son being lost altogether; had he publicly rebutted the

unfounded charge there and then, the
fraud must have been nipped in its in-
fancy, but probably the originators judged
that their victim would resort to what was
almost excusable under the circumstances,
namely, an escape; if so they too well
succeeded, as with Vincent Darecourt's
enforced absence the field lay open for the
full accomplishment of this unapproach-
able swindle."

All reference to the abstraction of the
letters from the Lord-Lieutenant was
carefully avoided.   The appearance of
Robert Arkwright in the witness-box
excited much comment amongst those who
recollected, or had heard of his career in
former days.   In a natural, easy, and un-
constrained manner he described his several
interviews with Dorrington Darecourt and
Brien Flynn, the purport of their conversation, and what was afterwards effected

in furtherance of the plans then mutually agreed upon; but his painful emotion when acknowledging to having signed the forged last will and testament of the late Lord, as published, in conjunction with Flynn, knowing the same to be false, and done for the purpose of defrauding Vincent of his legitimate inheritance, transferring it to his cousin, awoke great agitation, which became intensified by the nephew of the Darecourt agent swearing that the several deeds then in his hand, whereupon the claim of Dorrington was founded, were written by him in obedience to the mandate of his uncle. Producing this order, the witness pointed out that it bore a date rendering the existence of the will at the time specified an impossibility, the latter being antecedent to the former.

The short cross-examination in both instances only increased the weight of the given testimony, and a very appreciable conviction settled upon the assembly that the petitioner would establish her claim, notwithstanding the listless air of nonchalance assumed by the defendants. It was now observed in the heated chamber that the day had suddenly changed from sunshine . to darkness, foreshadowing a violent atmospherical commotion.

" Send for Flynn," said the male defendant authoritatively to his solicitor, " let him attend at once," and the trial proceeded.

" I do not know, my lord, that I need occupy the valuable time of the Court any longer ; " lifting a large bag full of parchments on to the green baize table, " here are the veritable titles to the disputed estate, the marriage settlement upon the late Lady Darecourt, and the will of her consort, confirming every iota that he had power over, real and personal, to their only son Vincent, the name of this surreptitious craven imposter, being wholly unknown or unacknowledged therein." The counsel then added, " Messrs. ———, solicitors for the petitioner, who also acted as legal representatives for the lords of Darecourt until its usurpation by this plain Mr. Dorrington Darecourt "—with emphasis—" will swear to the preparation and legal execution of these instruments; and this person," indicating Fanny, " presumptuously styling herself Lady Darecourt, can tell, if she wishes, how she failed in gaining possession of them last night—another phase of the fraudulent transaction—because that happily we were beforehand with her."

The energetic advocate was suddenly called outside just as the pent-up storm burst forth with startling fury.

"Close the windows and draw the curtains," exclaimed the Judge, every eye quailing before that blue livid flame traversing the Hall of Justice.

Ere the usher and others had had time to do as his lordship commanded, on came the redoubled peals of deafening sound which seemed to make the Court reel, while the concurrent flash of electric fluid was dazzling in its vivid power.

"My lord," proceeded the claimant's lawyer, speaking solemnly, "I have been summoned to the Hall to receive these papers, taken half-an-hour ago from the dead body of the agent and conspirator Brien Flynn;"—great sensation—"of course it is impossible to examine them at this moment; but I have read sufficient already to show that this evil man and his deceased servile confederate acted a cruel part indeed."

"Here," he went on, "are heart-broken letters, written by the late Lord Darecourt shortly before he expired to his only child" (Lucy was now much affected, while Sir Mervyn Mervyn bit his lips, angrily regarding the immovable defendants in front), "begging him to return home for a dying parent's blessing; again," he added, "I find a few strongly affectionate appeals from Vincent to his father, both of course having been intercepted by these guilty associates in a gross, audacious conspiracy, for which one has been deservedly cited to judgment on High, while the others await it at the bar of justice here, in your verdict of retributive impartiality to my defrauded, long-suffering client."

"My lord, my lord! stop that gentleman leaving the Court," passionately implored the male accused, pointing to the door whereat stood the unknown from Swords. "I cannot satisfactorily support my case," continued the supplicant, "in the absence of Brien Flynn, but at least I shall prove the legality of our union."

As the person indicated hesitatingly advanced to the Bench, the baronet earnestly searched his bronzed features, while Lucy having briefly looked towards him, turned her eyes listlessly away.

"My lord," observed the stranger in a fixed voice, "it will spare unnecessary details by my stating that I married these defendants, but I must respectfully decline to be sworn thereupon."

"We cannot permit of such trifling," responded the Judge in accents of rebuke.

"My lord, the ceremony took place on board ship several miles from the foreshore," was suggestively replied.

" But you did unite us ? " inquired the defendant.

" Yes ; I was constrained to go through that formulary."

" Is this your signature, Rev. Randall Massey ? " demanded the Judge, holding up the impounded, well-preserved certificate.

" It is, my Lord."

" Then why not be sworn upon it ? "

" Merely to spare this lady, my Lord," pointing to where Fanny stood.

" Spare the lady ! " resounded through the Hall, while she tottered to her seat.

" Cease this absurd comedy in presence of the Law, sir ! " came from the Bench 'mid growing excitement.

" My Lord," proceeded the reluctant witness, " the celebration of marriage was wrong on my side."

" Wrong ! " echoed the male defendant.

"Yes; I own it with regret. To save the life of my friend and myself, I went through the office, although I am not a clergyman."

Amid the ensuing tumult the dispenser of justice with great severity asked,—

"If you are not a clergyman, pray what may you lawfully be called?"

"A gentleman, my Lord."

All eyes are now concentrated upon that calm, long-bearded stranger.

"How do you reconcile such ignoble conduct, mocking a solemn ordinance, with that becoming in what you claim to be?"

"My Lord, it secured my friend's life and my own," hesitating.

"What more have you to add, sir?" angrily rejoined the aged Chief Justice.

"I promptly told the lady she was not honestly married, and that I regretted being coerced into the dissembling act."

" Who are you, miscreant ? " roared the astounded defendant Dorrington.

" Vincent Darecourt," came slowly and composedly in reply.

.CHAPTER XII.

GREAT and universal was the joy everywhere exhibited at the success of the petitioner in the memorable trial, heightened
as it became by the reuniting of Lucy and
her long-lost husband in such an unexpected manner.

From Dublin to Malahide and far down
the undulating coast bells rang out their
merry, tuneful peals at the result, while
adjoining the Darecourt estate triumphal
arches were erected in a marvellously short
time welcoming back its new and lawful
owners.

In friendly rivalry the tenantry of Sir

Mervyn Mervyn competed with their neigh-
bours, emulating the process of floral
greeting, and surely the best "bib and
tucker" were put on by the crowd passing,
—no, no, not passing the "Darecourt
Arms" until they have therein drunk the
health of the young Lord "and her bewtiful
leddyship," afterwards adding to that mass
of humanity surging towards the principal
entrance to the castle.

The well-known hostelrie was indeed *en
fête*, festoons and gaudy papers, inter-
spersed with branches of holly, being
promiscuously thrust in amid glittering
tin pots, yellow crockeryware, and ricketty,
disused barrels; while to the wonder of
conjecturing customers the venerated chair
was no longer left to its sleep of the
past, but banishing every particle of dust
therefrom, which could only have accrued
within the last few moments—Misthress

Gaffney had a habit of throwing her apron at it each time she passed—the landlord placed it in the position ordinarily occupied by himself, and henceforth it would become his nightly seat. Blatherbill never looked so profoundly happy as now, and oh, if a lie had to be manufactured, or some marvel concocted in a surprisingly short period, was he not in a mood to gratify the most sceptical? indeed, this redundancy of spirit at last, as he said to his wife, " dhrew the vint peg oud av his brain, an' he should tell her a narymative."

"Git a gon wid ye," she retorted, "ye innishint craythure, ye tould me a sthory the day I had the misforthin to let ye clap a ring an me finger, an' I must forgit that afore I belayve another."

The arrival of an enormous supply of spirituous liquid at this moment terminated the conjugal repartee, and doubtless spared the landlady the necessity of listening to her bluff spouse perpetrating the latest fabrication, for Blatherbill was very autocratic and absolute in securing attention during his favourite pastime.

" Av coorse the new lord 'ill pay for this sthock," suggested the purveyor's assistant, depositing the last instalment of that wide array of barrels and jars forming the " moighty ordher " from the " Darecourt Arms."

" Av coorse he won't be allowed to pay wan shmall farthin'," responded the landlord, assuming a tone and look of swelling importance.

" Begor the amount id destroy any man bud yersel, Misther Gaffney."

" Ay, an' I'd willin'ly rooin mesel' for sake av the tinder leddy comin' home today," was warmly volunteered.

It became evident, however, that his

better half did not appreciate this heroic abnegation, as she shouted from the other end of the shop,—

"Peter, yer lies 'ill be yer rooina-shun."

"Here they are, hurrah! hurrah!" rose up from a multitude of voices, and forgetting the ordinary assertion, "av havin id oud another time," Blatherbill waddled into the road to smoke his pipe, and present his " congratymilashuns " to the new lord and " leddy."

The vehicle of Sir Mervyn Mervyn in rich showy livery and ornate housings now approached, wherein sat Lucy look-ing pale and reflective, while her much-altered husband seemed to feel deeply the spontaneous welcome everywhere accorded to them. The baronet unmistakably en-joyed the scene; next to him being Eustace Dillon, dark, immovable, and impassible as though he lived without knowing or realizing existence.

The horses had been taken from the carriage, which was pulled along at a slow jog-trot by the many willing hands ever ready to assume their honoured former places. It could never be satisfactorily accounted for, how that in unspoken accord the equipage stopped opposite to the "Dare-court Arms," except that as the landlord was seen approaching with a grave air of importance, procedure became impossible until he had combed out whatever was troubling his brain, and certainly the thinker scratched his head with severity, resolving, " Now is me time to pordhuce a riputashun, av I only git a chance to knock a few shuparyor words into their impty nuts," when after a deep inspiration and polishing both hands in his apron, he commenced,—

" Leddy Darecoort an' yer unforthunate

husband,"—visible merriment in the carriage and concern among the crowd arrested his attention—" I beg yer pardon," he faltered confusedly, "I mayne—"

"Yer a liar, but yer not mayne," escaped from Cup-o'-Tay, who with Tom had been foremost in the equine occupation.

"In prisince av leddys, no wan shud tell trooth," retorted the would-be orator with marked seriousness.

Even Lucy joined in the enforced mirth attending this severe proof of pompous innocence; the only one who consistently declined to laugh was Blatherbill himself; however, believing it would be wiser to follow the general example, he tardily parted his lips, but still with such an obvious look of not understanding its cause that the amusement grew stronger against mine host.

Lord Darecourt resolved on coming to the rescue of the well-intentioned, floundering landlord, while Cup-o'-Tay's companion, Tom, determined on something else as he left the ranks of the procession and crossed the road.

"I am extremely grateful," said their new patron, "for this proof of your good feeling towards myself and Lady Darecourt; long may we continue to live on the same terms; and indeed nothing can be more likely, whilst you possess those sentiments towards us so eloquently expressed by my friend here," indicating the proprietor of the "Darecourt Arms."

In the earlier part of the noble speaker's felicitous remarks, Blatherbill stood savagely subdued, feeling appreciably that the Muses were from home when he had called upon them; but the instant his lordship designated him as his "elo-

quent friend," the pulse of the innkeeper
fired up with electrical effect.

"D'ye hear that," he shouted. "I'm
the frind of a rayl live lord, an' an illigant
sphaker beside."

"Oh, me lord, shake hands an id," he
plaintively urged, leaning half-way over
the vehicle in a hot perspiration, continuing, "av iver ye want a dhrink or a
noight's lodgin', don't pass the sign av
the—oh, holy murther, I'm kilt, I'm
dead," and the next instant Blatherbill lay
rolling like an elephant on the road,
while cheers and yells of delight rent the
air as the carriage was drawn forward,
its occupants being almost giddy with
recurring laughter.

Looking fixedly towards Lord Darecourt, with his arm outstretched, mine
host observed his lordship move recipro-
catingly towards him; but ah, what he

had grasped with the tightness of rapt delight could not be Lord Darecourt's hand, alas! no, it was the smithy's iron almost liquid in red heat, which Tom adroitly introduced at the right moment.

As his wife bent over him with her efficacious village nostrums, Blatherbill observed hopefully and emotionally,—

"Av I'm sphared now I'll niver tell another lie; niver, niver."

A joyous company are those assembled in Darecourt Castle when the hour is fast approaching midnight.

Vincent and Eustace had shown the false letters received by them representing Lucy as about to be married to the English baronet, now recognized as the creation of Fanny Chalmers, on the strength whereof her husband had written the reproachful missives produced by her assailant in Feltram Wood.

His recovery from supposed death was also accounted for, together with that mysterious appearance outside of the window at Howth and his subsequent jumping into the sea, being rescued therefrom by O'Grady.

Thus ruminating over the past, they speak of the present, Vincent and Mervyn cementing a friendship of bygone years by replete mutual explanations.

Publicly upbraiding his supposed wife with being the cause of their discomfiture, the false lord fled out of Court, abandoning her and his child. Lucy sent, offering to ameliorate the position of her former friend, who at all events was a mother, but during the evening there came a reply from the outcast of wormwood and gall effectually driving its author from further consideration.

It was the Outlaw who had tracked

Brien Flynn to the secret room under the Abbey, where he lay dead beneath that immense chest of gold, his manifest intention being to escape therewith whilst his confederates were detained in Court; but in poising it the mass overturned, and, a victim to deep-drawn avarice, his unjust life met with a meet reward, crushed by the weight of those dishonest accumulations.

Robert Arkwright and his wife are guests at Darecourt, looking happy and content in each other, although without children to bless their declining days, and as the clock points to half past eleven never was brighter, more unaffected joy than this radiating between those whom sorrow had chastened and adversity softened, thereby elevating them nearer to that standard of benevolent humility which has ere now characterized the greatest of mankind.

"How very odd," observed Lord Darecourt, "it wants but half an hour of midnight, yet O'Grady is absent."

"What will be our triumph, Vincent dear,
if he does not share it?" said his wife.

"His manner and words of last night
have seriously impressed me," continued
her noble husband, "as evidently pointing
to some great crisis in his career."

"I protest there shall be a crisis in his
career, the bravest, most disinterested
fellow in the whole world," exclaimed the
baronet warmly.

Lucy's eyes, already full of animation,
glowed anew as she affirmed,—

"I would cheerfully surrender all that I
possess or call mine own to secure his
happiness, not you of course"—to her
restored liege, who simulated a surprised
look,—"but I fear it will be impossible
to wean him from that resolve of living in

solitude, although, thanks to you, Sir Mervyn, the Government no longer desires his arrest."

" I want to escape from womankind for a year or two," volunteered the recipient of her thanks with an open smile, " why should we not both travel together ? "

" Her ladyship's estimate is well founded," interposed Arkwright, boldly, " I have known O'Grady from a boy, and rest assured that no human being can induce him to leave Ireland, or to forego his hermit-like life."

" Admirably spoken, and I thank you for the truthful words," came from the Outlaw himself, as unperceived he glided into their midst.

" Ah ! " inquired Lucy plaintively, " why leave us all these hours marvelling at your absence ? surely," she added reproachfully, " you might have given us a thought."

"Fire! fire! the castle's on fire!" now pealed through the building, while the sound of tumultuous voices and feet came rushing to the drawing-room, where all started up as the door was burst open and and the cries repeated.

"You are too late, my good people, go home content, the fire is extinguished," enjoined the patriot.

"We saw id jist this minnit, yer honour," was collectively and firmly pleaded.

"From the village you mean?"

"Yis, yer honour."

"My friends, in this well-intended ardour you forget the long uphill distance, but be satisfied, when you go back there will not be anything to alarm you," and the re-assured crowd with a cheer betook them-selves to enjoy the good things provided by Lord Darecourt.

"Which accounts for the prolonged

absence that we chided you upon," observed Lucy, "though the while you were as usual imperilling your life to save others."

"I tracked that false woman, Fanny Chalmers, to the basement of the castle, and silently watched her stack the materials for the incendiary exploit, which, when she had fired, I tossed to the winds, thereby doubtless awaking the consternation of the good people of the village."

"May she not find other means of injuring us?" asked the exalted hostess.

"None; having told me she had written to mislead you, I warned her never again to be seen near this place, or that I would reach her through her son. 'You hold your own existence valueless as it has proved worthless. But beware,' I urged; 'your child remains; foster it. There is no father left to acknowledge him now, do not disregard a mother's office. Twice you were spared—the next time you shall forfeit your son;' and I reached her maternal love, when the instinct of self was gone."

The wife of the Outlaw's noble host rose up impulsively, moving to him with outstretched hands, saying,—

"Another proof that Lucy Darecourt grows deeper your debtor hour by hour until the time has come when in justice she must ask you to blot out this compound obligation by—"

"Mistress of Darecourt," he interrupted with a dignity and solemnity of word and manner that awed his observers, as, shaking the locks back from his massive forehead, he looked with a pensive glance into Lucy's full expectant face, "take from me the last sacred impress of affection's benediction,"—kissing her forehead,—"it is the poor rebel's only patrimony, and never more will human joy be mine, although contentment may bless my wearied eyes before they close in their final sleep. In the days to come, when remembering him whom you once have known, it were best to think he is at peace, although his distracted soul is weary with the unequal struggle against separation from all he ever loved or cherished. An unnatural contest, wherein death alone can prove the victor, the welcome end of a long life's hazard to him now known no more as the lonely Outlaw of Wentworth Waste."

The agitated enthusiast abruptly rushed from the room, while his auditors remained transfixed in dumb emotion.

Recovering herself, Lady Darecourt ran to the window, which she forced wide open, calling aloud towards that shrouded, black avenue in front,—

" Come back !—I conjure you !—by the

memory of your dead mother's love, of Ireland's green sainted hills, the land you served so nobly, do not leave us," and they stood silently listening, while each bosom suspended its lifelong action.

The cold, cruel night-wind at last floated upwards from the far end of that dense tree-clad walk, bearing the mournful dirge, " No more! no more!!" and ever afterwards, while all of those now assembled in heart-broken sorrow at that casement, survived, fighting life's fitful battle of joy or strife, they neither saw nor heard again of Michael O'Grady.

THE END.